THE DEVIL'S MISTRESS

A REGENCY ROMANCE

VILLAIN'S REDEMPTION SERIES
BOOK ONE

WREN ST CLAIRE

THE DEVIL'S MISTRESS
A REGENCY ROMANCE

WREN ST CLAIRE

Egyptian
Mysteries

Created with Vellum

❦ Created with Vellum

CHAPTER 1

The gentleman's arm tightened at the lady's waist, as he moved her effortlessly round the dance floor to the tune of the Viennese Waltz.

"Do you remove immediately from town?" he asked twirling her elegantly.

"By the end of the week my Lord." She said with a flash of her magnificent blue eyes as she turned her head on a graceful neck, glossy black ringlets bobbing with the movement.

"And where will you be spending Christmas?" he asked recapturing her in his embrace.

She flung her head back to look up at him "At Belmont with my uncle's family" she said then dropped her eyes demurely and added "Unless I receive another offer."

He pulled her closer as they turned with the music. "That could be arranged Miss Torrington." He said with a meaningful squeeze.

Her hand on his upper arm gave a momentary pressure, to keep her balance no doubt. "You will have to apply to my uncle, Sir" she said with a sideways look that was as captivating as it was teasing.

"Tomorrow at twelve." he said. "You will be at home?" She met the intensity of his stare with a considering look. And then she smiled "I believe I may, Lord Stanton."

LADY MARY WROXTON watched her brother leading Miss Viviana Torrington through the waltz and sighed. She thought they were the best-looking couple in the room. Miss Torrington was an accredited beauty with fashionably dark hair, stunningly large, long-lashed eyes, striking features, including a perfectly shaped mouth, a lovely jaw line, swan-like neck and a tall slender, well-proportioned figure. Mary knew herself to be partial; however, there was no denying that her brother was an excellent partner. He made an impressive figure, being tall and well-formed, with broad shoulders that did not require padding, a trim waistline and muscular legs that showed the prevailing fashion of skin-tight pantaloons to advantage. Turning to her spouse she tapped his sleeve with her fan.

"Wroxton, don't they make a handsome couple?"

"Eh?" said Lord Wroxton starting out of a brown study. She waved her fan at the pair. "Denzil and Viviana!"

"Oh aye! Very pretty!" said Wroxton. "Though if you ask me, she's got too much vivacity by half!"

"Wroxton! How can you say so?" said Lady Mary indignantly "Her manners are lively to be sure, but nothing beyond the line of what is pleasing!"

Wroxton snorted. "Miss Torrington is an outrageous flirt! What do you think she is doing now?"

"She has a partiality for Denzil I am persuaded!" protested Lady Mary

"Yes, and half the other eligibles she has making cakes of themselves over her too!" responded Wroxton with a sardonic smile.

"Denzil is not making a cake of himself!" said Denzil's loyal sister firmly. "He has by far too much address to be doing anything of the sort! And in any case," she added as if this were a clincher. "He is far and away the most attractive of her suitors, I am quite certain she could not prefer Avon, or Bentley or even Harcourt over him!"

"I don't know!" said Wroxton "If she's a fancy to be a Duchess or a Marchioness rather than a mere Countess...."

"Wroxton you are teasing me!" said Lady Mary rapping his arm with her fan again. "She positively could not prefer that middle-aged fop Avon over Denzil even if he is a Duke! As for Bentley, he hasn't the least style, why I swear he had gravy stains on his waistcoat at the Gatling's dinner dance the other night!"

"Very well, but you must admit Harcourt has the inside running. The bets are two to one at Whites in his favour."

Lady Mary sniffed. "Gentlemen are perfectly odious. I hope you haven't been indulging in such vulgarity Timothy!"

He smiled down at her. "No, I've no desire to lose my blunt, besides, it wouldn't be seemly for me to bet against Denzil."

"You can't mean you really think Denzil will lose out to Harcourt?" protested Mary, opening her pale blue eyes wider.

For answer Wroxton nodded his head in the direction of the persons they were discussing.

The waltz had finished and the Earl of Stanton had led his lovely partner off the dance floor, but before he could restore her to her grandmother, Lady Hartley, they were intercepted by a tall solidly built gentleman with hair as red as a flame.

SIR ANTHONY HARCOURT BOWED SUAVELY.

"You will allow me to relieve you of your lovely burden Stanton. I believe the next dance is mine Miss Torrington."

"True Sir Anthony, but you are a little previous, it will not commence for at least ten minutes and I would like a mite of refreshment first," replied Miss Torrington.

Stanton detected the tremble of her fingers on his arm, caught the taught undertone in her voice, and was alerted instantly to her distress. He glanced from her slightly flushed face to the overly bright light in Harcourt's deep blue eyes as they rested on her. Harcourt was possessed of the very rare combination of dark red hair and black eyebrows. His features were strongly hand-some. He was known as a hardened gamester, rumoured to have lost and regained more than one fortune at play. From Stanton's perspective he was a ruthless devil with a shocking reputation. It would seem from her demeanour that Miss Torrington was angry with him about something. All to the good as far as Stanton was concerned. Suppressing a smile, he added fuel to the fire by saying, "Perhaps you can retrieve your position by fetching the lady a glass of Ratafia, Sir?"

Harcourt threw him a savage glance and nodded, bowing punctiliously to Miss Torrington. "Certainly, if that is your desire, Miss Torrington?"

She nodded imperiously, and he turned away making his way across the crowded ballroom to the refreshments that were laid out in a separate chamber.

"Has Sir Anthony done something to upset you, Miss Torrington?"

She laughed but it sounded forced. "Good heavens no, what ever gave you that impression my Lord?"

He looked down at her steadily, gently. "I would hope that you would trust me enough to confide in me my dear. I also hope that you know I am yours to command. If Harcourt troubles you –"

"So chivalrous my Lord. Are you offering to be my champion?" she said lightly.

"Are you never serious?" he chided, smiling to soften the words.

She lowered her lashes demurely. "You may find me more sober tomorrow, my Lord." She raised her eyes sparkling with mischief. "Tonight, I am too gay for that!"

"Miss Torrington, your drink." Harcourt proffered the wine glass, which she took with a nod and a cool glance.

"I thank you Sir." Over it she glanced at Stanton and then away, clearly dismissing him.

Stanton stepped back, allowing himself to be ousted. A ballroom was no place for a show of possessiveness. In any case she had as good as told him what her answer would be. Perhaps she proposed to let Harcourt down gently? Observing that gentleman's fiery expression, he doubted the man would take it well.

Stanton retired to a safe distance to watch the proceedings. Miss Torrington sipped her wine and responded to something her companion said with a toss of her head. Miss Torrington was clearly not happy with Sir Anthony. Stanton smiled.

"What are you so pleased about Den?" drawled a familiar voice in his ear. "Ah the little Torrington. Gad man you're a dog with a bone. The clubs are all betting that she'll have Harcourt in the end. The old man won't last too much longer they say."

"Ashley, I find your conversation offensive. In any case, you're wrong."

"No, no my dear fellow. Had it from Granville last week, the old boy is on his last legs. Swear he won't live past Christmas. Once Harcourt has the title and the estate, there'll be no stopping him. She won't turn down the chance to be a Duchess."

Stanton looked round at his lanky companion, a thin faced gentleman dressed with careless elegance. "Damn it Ash, if you weren't my friend, I'd give you one in the jaw for speaking of Miss Torrington like that."

"Den, you have become a dead bore since you fell in love. I swear, you've even lost your sense of humour," complained the Honourable Ashley Morton.

Stanton ignored him and scanned the room realising that the object of his obsession was nowhere in sight. Nor could he see the tell-tale red hair of Sir Anthony. The next set was forming, the dance would commence within moments. He waited only until the musicians struck up. Certain that Miss Torrington was not among the dancers, he edged his way round the ballroom towards the door to the refreshment room. Scanning that room, he found no sign of his quarry. There were doors at the end that led to the retiring rooms and one that led to a gallery which ran along the side of the ballroom. Surely, she had too much sense than to allow Harcourt to take her into the Gallery? It was most improper, and frankly dangerous. Harcourt, in Stanton's opinion, could not be trusted to keep the line.

He crossed the room and stepped into the Gallery. It was not deserted, there were a few couples strolling or seated on sofa's positioned at various points along the length of the long narrow room. But a quick reconnoitre told him that Miss Torrington was not of their number. He returned to the refreshment room and was gratified by the sight of Miss Torrington emerging from the ladies retiring room. Of her erstwhile companion there was no sign. Relieved he decided against advertising his presence to her. He didn't particularly wish to appear in the light of an overprotective lover. He hoped that he might soon have the right to play such a role. But until then it was better not to cram his fences. Miss Torrington was incredibly light at hand. He didn't wish to queer his pitch.

"Do you wish to dance Miss Torrington?"

Viviana tossed a curl back from her shoulder. "I think not Sir Anthony."

"You are contrary tonight, Miss Torrington."

She sipped her wine coolly. "A woman's prerogative, Sir Anthony."

"A turn about the gallery instead?" he asked eating her with his eyes. She shivered and struggled with herself. It would not be seemly to walk in the gallery with him, or any gentleman. She was tempted, she badly wanted to quarrel with him, and doing it in public wasn't possible.

"You're angry with me, what about?" he said abruptly.

She finished her wine, handed the glass to a hovering waiter, and walked off. He followed her to the curtained doorway that led to the gallery.

She stepped through and glanced around. There was a couple at the other end of the gallery, but they appeared occupied with one another. Sir Anthony took her arm and she allowed him to guide her to a couch situated between two pillars. She sat, and he seated himself beside her. "Tell me what I have done to anger you, Miss Torrington."

She twitched the train of her ball gown and glanced at him sideways. He appeared perfectly at ease, his earlier annoyance seemed to have faded, replaced by an air of slight amusement. This made her even angrier. "It has come to my attention Sir Anthony, that certain bets are being laid in the gentleman's clubs."

He raised one dark eyebrow. "What indiscreet person told you that?"

"It is of no importance who told me! Is it true?"

"I can understand your annoyance over the matter Miss Torrington, I fail to comprehend your anger with me," he responded.

"Because Sir Anthony, *I* understand that you have wagered a large sum on yourself to win!" she snapped.

"Miss Torrington, you have been misled" he replied evenly.

"Then it is not true?" she asked.

"I am a gamester Miss Torrington, but I am not a fool."

She scanned his face for the truth. "What am I to believe Sir Anthony? That I have been the victim of a trouble-making gossip?"

"The betting is true enough, but I have had no part in it."

She flushed with fury, snapped open her fan and applied it vigorously. "Men are despicable!"

He looked down carefully. "No doubt. I might even be

7

included in that number, but in this case, I am innocent of the crime accused."

She snapped her fan shut and stood up. "Thank you for your honesty. Sir Anthony. I think we should return to the ballroom now. My grandmother will be looking for me." The other couple had left the gallery, and they were alone.

He rose and took her hand, saying, "Momentarily my dear. May I -" she looked up at him as he bent and kissed her hand. It was an old-fashioned courtly gesture, generally reserved these days for older married women, or members of one's family.

His other arm circled her waist and drew her against his chest before she realised what he was about. She put a hand on his chest to push him away

"Sir -"

He lowered his head and kissed her full on her mouth. His lips were soft and warm and a rush of sensation flooded her body as his lips moved over hers, persuasive. She froze, shocked as much by her own response as his kiss. He released her quickly, and she stared up at him dazed.

It was quite improper and rather thrilling of him to kiss her. A flutter in her stomach sent a bolt of something warm and exciting diving down her belly as he held her eyes with his, and said softly, "Miss Torrington, I have a hard head, but you are strong wine for any man. Intoxicating, even for a jaded palate such as mine. If I should call tomorrow afternoon, will I find you at home?"

She flushed again and this time with another emotion.

She felt confused and off balance, less than half an hour ago she had virtually promised Stanton she would accept his suit. Did she mean to do so? She was still unsure. She used to think Stanton dull, but he was a better match on all counts than any other. He wasn't a fortune hunter, and he was a thorough gentleman. Sir Anthony on the other hand…. There was no denying this man's attraction. He was handsome and tantalisingly enigmatic, dangerous. Something in his eyes called to her blood and sent a shiver of apprehension down her spine.

She extricated her hand from his and picked up her train turning away. She spoke over her shoulder as she walked towards the doorway, back into the refreshment room. "I hardly know Sir Anthony, my calendar is so full I dare swear I have a dozen engagements for tomorrow afternoon." She swept through the doorway and headed towards the ladies' room at a rapid clip. As she reached the screen, she glanced back over shoulder, but he hadn't followed her. With a fast-beating heart she disappeared behind the screen.

A PRECISELY TWELVE noon the following day Stanton presented himself at Belfort House, the town residence of Lord Belfort, Miss Torrington's maternal uncle and her guardian. Viviana Torrington was not only a beautiful young woman she was also an heiress. Being the fortunate possessor of the holy triumvirate of birth, beauty and wealth, she had been the reigning Queen of the Ton since her debut in April of that year. During the seven months since that advent, she had received (it was rumoured) no less than a dozen proposals of marriage. To her grandmother's eternal exasperation and her uncle's bewilderment, she had to date refused every one of them. Several of her suitors had not allowed the initial rebuff to snuff out their hopes, and they continued to dance attendance on her. She seemed not to object to this. She divided her favours amongst them and seemingly refused to take any of them seriously.

Stanton himself had not entered the lists until the commencement of the little season in September. Finding himself seated beside the beauty at a dinner one evening he was enchanted by her unusual conversation. Intrigued he pursued the acquaintance and in a very short space of time was forced to the conclusion that he, like every other male in London, had fallen under her spell.

Shown into the parlour, where a fire burned merrily to take the chill off the elegantly furnished apartment, he was not kept waiting long. Belfort a middle-aged, portly gentleman with a round face and thinning hair, closed the door with a careless backhand and crossed the room his right hand held out in welcome.

"Stanton! Well by Jove, what a pleasant occurrence. Can I guess what errand brings you here?"

"You might well, my Lord, it most nearly concerns your niece," said Stanton shaking hands with his host.

"Well, I am sure I wish you all the best my boy and I would that I could promise you a positive outcome, but I dare not. I've presented a dozen offers to her, and she's not accepted any of them. It has me in a puzzle what she wants! Not that I'd have had her accept the first offer she was made, but a dozen?" he shook his head "It's become embarrassing my boy!"

Stanton, who had not been referred to as a boy since he was in short coats, concealed his mild irritation. "Are you trying to tell me my suit will not prosper Lord Belfort?"

"Oh no, not at all! I Certainly hope it does, but I cannot promise you that it will! I fear she has more of her mother in her than we would like, but there, Heloise was always headstrong! I shall fetch her, and she can tell you herself whether she'll have you or not. I'm sure I can't tell." He bustled out of the room leaving Stanton to ponder what his fate might be.

Five minutes later the door opened again and Stanton turned from the fire to greet his lady love. She paused inside the door and looked at him speculatively. He noted that she did not appear in the least shy or agitated. But then, if she had received a dozen offers, he supposed she must be accustomed to it. She was tastefully attired in a morning dress of white cambric and a navy spencer.

She came towards him and dropped a neat curtsy. "You are punctual my Lord."

He took her hand. "That is generally held to be one of my traits. How do you do this morning, are you quite recovered from last night's frivolities?"

"Oh yes, it takes more than a ball to knock me up!" she said lightly.

He had retained hold of her hand and she had made no attempt to retrieve it. Emboldened he said, "You know why I am here, my dear, what is it to be? Will you accept my hand and heart or send me away with my tail between my legs?"

"What no romantic gestures? I fancy you are supposed to kneel when making a proposal my Lord."

"Did your previous suitors kneel?" he asked with a quizzing look. She was playing with him, and while that might annoy him, he wasn't going to show it.

"Oh yes!" she said with a mischievous smile.

"Well, it didn't do them any good did it?" he replied with complete sangfroid.

She sighed and glanced at him under her lashes. "Are you not going to make any attempt to persuade me of the advantages of the match, my Lord?"

"No. If they are not self-evident, I've no intention of making myself sound like a coxcomb enumerating them."

"Then how do you expect your suit to prosper?" she said her voice unsteady with laughter.

"Have done with your nonsense, Viviana! I love you. Do you love me?" he said bluntly.

"I hardly know my Lord!" she replied. "When you have not so much as kissed me!"

"You are an unprincipled baggage!" he said taking her in his arms.

"Yes, I know!" she said with an encouraging smile. "Quite

sunk below reproach! Are you sure you want me for your Countess Denzil?"

His response to this final sally was to kiss her. Thoroughly. Releasing her mouth some little while later he said a trifle unsteadily. "Is that sufficient answer Viviana my darling?"

His eyes rested on her flushed countenance, and he had the satisfaction of knowing he had finally pierced her armour. "Good heavens Denzil, yes!" she said as breathless as he. "I had no idea you could be so –"

"Passionate?" he asked his eyes devouring her beauty. "My wife won't want for attention my dear."

Recovering her poise, a little, she laughed. "I was going to say persuasive. But passionate is a better word. You always behave so properly, I wondered...."

"So, the secret to winning your heart is to stop behaving like a gentleman, is that it?" he asked, tightening his hold.

She hesitated and then said, "Not precisely. The truth is, I was used to think you rather dull. I am a sad rattle Denzil. Easily bored and shockingly flirtatious, are you sure you can handle me?"

"Are you still funning love? When will you be serious?" he said caressingly.

She searched his eyes anxiously. "I'm afraid you're too good for me Denzil. I'll lead you a merry dance, you know that don't you?"

"What nonsense you do talk sweetheart!"

She leaned her cheek upon his shoulder and said softly, "Oh Denzil I shall try to be good, for you deserve nothing less!"

"My little love." He said foolishly against her hair.

She lifted her face and he kissed her again. Her arms went round his neck, and she kissed him back. Belatedly it occurred to him to wonder what her uncle had meant about the reference to her mother. Some vague memory of scandal teased him, but its substance eluded him. He shrugged it off, too happy with the outcome of his proposal to concern himself with something that was no doubt ancient history.

CRAWLING between the sheets that evening, Viviana reflected on a day that had changed her life irrevocably. She had not known that she would accept Denzil's offer that morning, yet with him before her, and regarding her with his frank eyes and honest avowal of love she had not been able to resist. A sudden hankering for steadiness had seized her and his kiss... She touched her lips and nestled into the pillows with a sensuous wiggle. She had not known he could kiss like that. The kiss had brought her wavering to a standstill.

She had always known she could never marry a man she felt no attraction for. Even if her mother's example had not taught her that, she thought her own nature would have prompted it. She craved excitement and passion like a flower craved water and sunlight. But she needed soil too, and Denzil would provide that. She knew that it was not uncommon for a lively woman to marry a staider man, Denzil would be her anchor, stop her from becoming completely irredeemable–if that were possible, given her history.

Dark memories loomed and she pushed them away resolutely. She would not dwell on the past, especially now when she had so much to look forward to. She had to marry someone, and he loved her so. Denzil's pure love would keep her safe from the demon's that lurked in her soul.

She rolled onto her stomach and closed her eyes. She would spend Christmas at his country house, and they would get to know each other better. They had barely spent any time alone, really alone since they met. She rather thought she might enjoy being gently seduced by Denzil...

...*you are strong wine for any man. Intoxicating...* She opened her eyes and stared at the shadowed wall, feeling a shiver of something between fear and desire in her belly. There was a man who called to the darkness in her. *Had she chosen the right man?*

She closed her eyes firmly. Of course, she might toy with the idea of marrying the devil, but she was better off with Denzil, much better off.

As she drifted into slumber, she wondered what Sir Anthony had made of her *not* being at home this afternoon and what she would say to him the next time they met.

CHAPTER 2

There was a loud crash and Anne Harcourt flinched, her heart thumping with sickening dread.

"Anne!" the voice bellowed from below.

Resisting the urge to pull the covers over her head and feign sleep, deafness or death, Anne got up and pulled on her dressing gown and a thick shawl against the arctic temperature in the room. The fire had died and the winter weather was rapidly closing in. Pushing her slender feet into slippers, she took up her night candle and ventured out to the hall as far as the top of the stairs. A lamp on the side table in the vestibule below showed her a rain sodden man's riding coat hanging carelessly over the newel post of the staircase and the damp marks of wet boots on the carpet.

The door of the front room, loosely referred to as the library, stood open and the light from several candles threw a cross-shadow overlapping with that of the lamp on the carpet. Old Newell the butler was deaf as a post and would not have heard either her brother's entrance nor his urgent summons. Hence the bellow for her attention.

With a sigh, she descended the stairs and entered the room,

clutching the shawl round her thin shoulders and trying to resist the urge to shiver. The room, lit by a single candelabra on the mantle shelf above the fireplace was dark, the impression increased by the addition of heavy furniture and wood panelling. Her father's duelling swords above the mantle glittered in the flickering light of the candle flame.

A large man in riding dress was attempting to light a fire in the grate. He swung round at her entrance and scowled at her, the sour expression marring what objectively could be described as harshly handsome features. His hair was slicked down with damp, which turned its normal flame colour to a rich ruddy brown. "There you are. Light this will you? Have the servants all deserted their posts?"

Anne came forward obediently, taking the taper from him and rearranging the kindling with one hand. Her voice was mild as she said, "No they are merely asleep. No one was expecting you tonight. Besides, you know Newell is stone deaf."

Having set the kindling appropriately, she re-ignited the fire and coaxed the flame to take. Kneeling in front of the hearth in her dressing gown, she was aware of Anthony's gaze on her but ignored it. He was in a foul temper, but there was nothing unusual in that. She was thankful that he didn't appear to be drunk and wondered what had brought him home from London so suddenly and in such a foul mood.

He had poured himself a generous serving of brandy and was drinking it with studied concentration. The fire was well alight now, so she stood. "Is there anything else you require?"

He stuck his feet out. "Yes, remove my boots, they're wet through, it's miserable outside, and I've been riding for hours."

Anne bent to the task of removing the sodden and muddy boots, attempting to avoid getting mud on her dressing gown. It did not so much as cross her mind to summon his man to perform the task. She knew perfectly well why he asked her to do such thing's for him, it was part of the contract. The contract to care for him and his household, since she had retired from the marriage mart unwed and become a burden on his purse.

Since his boots were well cut and an extremely good fit, it was not an easy task, but by dint of working the boot from the heel she was able to get first one and then the other off. Setting them down before the fire to dry she straightened and moved to leave him, but he called her back. Turning in the doorway she looked an enquiry.

"How is the old man, have you heard?"

"Aunt Amelia writes that apart from the gout and a bad dose of temper he has recovered from the apoplexy and seems like to survive for good while yet, why?"

"I think you should visit him for Christmas." He said pursing his lips thoughtfully. "Dutiful granddaughter and all that."

"Good heavens he would wish me at the very devil!" exclaimed Anne, fully alive to the foulness of her grand sire's temper, which was every bit as bad as her brother's. It was a Harcourt trait that seemed to go hand in hand with the red hair. She was the only member who seemed to have escaped the twin curse. Red hair but no temper, or at least she owned, one that she could curb.

"Nonsense, you're the only one of us he can stand. In fact, you're his favourite."

"How do you come by that conclusion?" she could feel her expression curdling derisively.

Anthony sipped his brandy and eyed her over the glass. "He told me. Last time we had a turn up."

She shook her head "I am persuaded he was bamming you. I am by far too poor a creature. He prefers those who stand up to him and his foul temper always puts me in a quake, you know it does."

"I don't know that Annie, he was in a maudlin fit, said you reminded him of Elizabeth." He drained his glass and refilled it from the decanter beside his chair.

Anne blinked at this unexpected comparison with a long dead Aunt. "Well, I can't credit it."

"Oh, stop twittering, Annie, it's one of your worst habits. No wonder no man of sense will have you."

Anne flushed and lowered her eyes reflecting that it was a fortunate circumstance for the harmony of the household that she at least had not inherited the family temper. His barbs rolled off, deflected by an internal defence mechanism long exercised against his thoughtless cruelty. To say she was accustomed to it, would be a mild understatement. She was so inured to his sharp temper that she didn't hear the half of it, at least not consciously. It was a habit developed in childhood against their parents incessant fighting.

"No wait, there was Gradley sniffing round your skirts, but you frightened him off. I could never fathom why. He was handsome enough and had a respectable fortune. You could have had your own household and a parcel of babies by now. Instead, you let him marry the Braydon chit. What ailed you?"

Anne flushed scarlet her heart thudding rapidly with panicked embarrassment.

"He never asked me Anthony."

He narrowed his eyes at her. "He was going to I'd swear it then something made him sheer off. I'd have sworn you were in love too, for you were swoony and moody, forever bursting into tears."

"I was eighteen Anthony!" She protested.

"If it wasn't Gradley that inspired all that missishness, what was it? Who -?"

"No one, you are quite mistaken in your recollections."

"Am I?" he regarded her in silence and her colour rose even further as she fidgeted with the buttons on her night gown.

He wasn't mistaken she had done everything she could to discourage Lord Gradley from his dogged pursuit of her. How could she have accepted an offer from a man she couldn't love, when her heart was given to another who didn't even know she was alive? She hadn't seen Denzil Elliot in years and the flame she had nursed as a girl had become a banked ember, but it had never been extinguished. She did not intend for her brother to get wind of it, for he would take great delight in snuffing it out for her.

Instead, she said mendaciously, "I wasn't of the belief that you wished any man — of sense or otherwise, to have me — after all it would be quite uncomfortable without me to order the household as you like it."

He glared at her over the rim. "I am in expectation of taking a wife soon. Which will make you not only redundant, but de trop."

Her colour deepened and she said a little unsteadily.

"Good God Tony what woman of breeding would have you?"

He leaned forward and the flash in his eyes made her step back involuntarily. His hand tightened on the chair arm and after a moment he said softly, "I will pretend you didn't say that." He sat back. "Instead, you will oblige me by visiting our grand sire for Christmas and making yourself agreeable to him. I will accompany you."

"I thought the last time you saw him, he swore he wouldn't have you in the house?" objected Anne with a wide-eyed innocent look.

His lips thinned. "I trust your memory is better than his."

SIR ANTHONY WATCHED his sister leave the room with a mixture of irritation and guilt. He had been harsher than he had meant to be, but she touched him on the raw, and he was angry, angrier than he could remember being in a while. He returned his gaze morosely to the fire, tossing off the brandy in his glass and refilling it. His carefully laid plans were in tatters and his creditors, scenting his loss, were becoming more and more pressing. He was rapidly running out of options.

He had long resisted the idea of seeking a solution to his financial difficulties through marriage, he preferred to restore his fortunes at the gaming table. The risk and the thrill, appealed to his need to pit his wits against an opponent and win. But his legendary luck had eluded him for over a year now and his existence had become precarious.

Then Viviana Torrington had appeared on his horizon and for the first time he was tempted. The lady was not only a considerable heiress, she was also beautiful. But not even that attractive combination would have tempted him if she had not also been possessed of a spirit that he recognised as kindred.

Viviana was a lady born, but something in her makeup was awry, he sensed it, and it made his pulse quicken in a way that was as disturbing as it was enjoyable. She wanted, no she needed something that Stanton, could never give her. He knew with certainty that this union was flawed. Stanton would never satisfy her. But would she realise it too late? And how was he to rescue her from her mistake, when she was to be buried at Stanton's country seat for the better part of the winter?

He should have kissed her properly, not just a touch of the lips but a deep exploratory kiss that would have set her ablaze. He could see the potential of it lying dormant in her eyes. He had refrained from a fear of losing control and frightening her off. She had been properly raised, but for all that, a dangerous desire smouldered beneath the surface waiting to be awoken. It spoke to him so strongly, he was unsure that if he kissed her properly, and she responded in kind, he would be able to stop.

He drank his brandy and cursed inwardly. If he had kissed her with the ravishing heat he wanted to unleash, wakened that slumbering desire, he could have made her his. He was sure of it. He lost himself momentarily in the fantasy of possessing her and frustrated desire made him angrier than ever. He wasn't used to being thwarted. What he couldn't obtain through charm he usually got by force of will. It was a facer to be set back on his heels like this.

His only comfort was that Stanton was too cold-blooded to rouse her, and too boring to hold her interest. She would tire of him, but how soon? And how could he hasten that end before she got herself tied to Stanton irrevocably?

He stared morosely into the fire and reflected on his words with Anne, she had been in love with somebody, more fool her. How she could entertain the possibility of love, having been raised as they both were in the war zone of their parents' passionate hatred of each other he didn't know. But then Anne was of a sweeter nature than he. His mind roamed back eight years to Anne's season trying to identify who the focus of her schoolgirl crush could have been.

"Good God!" he laughed. "Damn it Anne, you foolish girl!"

CHAPTER 3

"*J*ack!" squealed Lady Mary, regardless of her dignity, tumbling down the stairs into the arms of the handsome officer standing in the vestibule of Seven Oaks, the country seat of the House of Elliot, and the Earl of Stanton. "How did you get here?" she said being lifted off her dainty slipper shod feet for a bear hug.

"By post of course pea-goose!" exclaimed Captain Jack Elliot. "You look well Mary."

"Oh yes, I am most happy!" she said smiling delightedly. "Jack are you home permanently or is this just a visit?"

"If Boney stays put, I hope it's permanent. I've just lately quit the Congress of Vienna. The diplomats were still prosing on, but the bulk of the work has been done, and I was finally given leave to go. You have no idea how relieved I was. I'd rather face hordes of French soldiers than listen to politicians drone on for hours. The last three months have been nothing but torture!" Captain Jack, aka The Honourable John Francis Elliot, was twenty-six years of age and had been serving in Spain in his majesties Dragoon Guards for more than two years.

"Jack it so wonderful to have you home, come into the sitting room and tell me all about it."

"Devil take it Mary, let me put off my dirt first."

"Welcome home Master Jack!" said a voice behind him, and he turned to shake the hand of his brothers Butler. "Porth! I am glad to be home!" A man came in the front door carrying two bags and Jack waved at him. "Porth this is my batman Hardy, please show him to my room and make accommodations for him, will you?"

"I will that Master Jack. And may I say on behalf of the staff that we are right glad you're home and in one piece Sir!"

"Jack, you devil! Where did you spring from?" The Earl of Stanton emerged from the library and strode towards his brother, hands held out in welcome. "I wondered what all the noise was about!"

"Den! You look fit as be damned. Not worn out with the social round I see?" the two men who were much of a height, although Jack was a smidgen taller and broader than his brother, embraced affectionately.

"You might have warned us Jack."

"No why? Besides I barely had time. Right up until the last I was sure I was going to be stuck in Vienna for Christmas. By the time I knew I had leave, any letter I sent would arrive at the same time I did." His eyes wandered past his brother's shoulder and were arrested by the sight of two ladies he didn't know. One was a short, round, elderly lady with vague eyes and a kind mouth and the other was simply the most beautiful girl he had ever seen.

Stanton seeing the direction of his gaze, turned and brought the ladies forward. Saying, "Jack I would like to make you known to Lady Hartley and her granddaughter, my affianced bride, Miss Viviana Torrington. This is my brother Captain John Elliot, but we all call him Jack."

The captain made both ladies an elegant bow addressing the

older lady first. "Lady Hartley, delighted to make your acquaintance."

Lady Hartley smiled up at him, for she was very short. "My dear young man the delight is all mine!" He kissed her hand and turned his gaze to the beauty.

"Enchanted Miss Torrington." He took her hand and then with a cheeky smile said, "My brother has been remiss in informing me of this felicitous news. But may I encroach on the relationship to kiss your cheek my dear? You will be my sister after all."

This charming speech seemed to meet with Miss Torrington's approval since she offered her cheek. "Indeed, if you will let me call you Jack like the rest of the family?" she said with one of her dazzling smiles.

Jack kissed her cheek. "I wouldn't hear of anything else, Viviana." He looked over her head at his brother. "Den, you complete hand, why didn't you tell me?"

"Keep your shirt on Jack. It's only just happened, and in any case, I did tell you. But presumably you posted home before you received my missive."

"Well, I wish you every happiness, you old dog! Come upstairs with me and tell me all about it, I am agog to know!" said Jack with smooth aplomb. He bowed again to the ladies. "Lady Hartley, Mary, Viviana, if you will excuse me, I must change and look forward very much to furthering my acquaintance!"

Seizing his brother's arm, Jack virtually hauled the Earl up the stairs saying over his shoulder, "I assume my old room is still mine Porth?"

"Indeed Master Jack, a maid shall be sent straight to make up the room for you."

Jack waved a hand in acknowledgement and disappeared with his brother into the upper regions.

. . .

THE EARL LAUGHED as Jack shut the door to his room behind them. "Jack you are as precipitate still as a thunderstorm!"

"I precipitate?" said Jack surveying his room, which was pretty much as he remembered it. "Good God sober sides, you have succeeded in taking my breath away!"

"Have I indeed?" said the Earl much entertained. "That is certainly an achievement! I gather you approve of my engagement?"

"Approve? I'm stunned. I doubt if I have ever seen a more beautiful girl!"

"Yes, she has countenance, doesn't she?" said the Earl seating himself in the only armchair the room boasted.

"Countenance?" expostulated Jack

"And elegance of style. And a lively disposition and sense of humour. When I tell you that she is well-born and an heiress to boot you will perceive I have done well for myself."

"I hardly need ask this, but do you love her?"

The Earl's expression softened. "To distraction Jack. She is — perfect!"

Jack digested this. After a moment he said "Well no fellow deserved happiness more, I am delighted for you Den."

"Thank you. I own to some feelings of disbelief. I might be in danger of becoming set up in my own esteem Jack! She had received no less than twelve offers of marriage before mine. I am still not certain why she accepted me above all the rest."

Jack looked sharply at him. "Good heavens Den, why would she not? A better man does not exist. She is fortunate indeed to have captured your affection."

"As I am to have captured hers. I am so glad you have come home Jack. I've missed you. And I am sure you will deal extremely with Viviana, she has just your sense of humour and playfulness."

A knock at the door heralded the arrival of both Hardy and the chamber maid.

The Earl left his brother and descended to the drawing room where he found Lady Hartley, his sister, his betrothed and his brother-in-law. Mary was still exclaiming over Jacks arrival and her spouse was saying as Denzil entered the room, "Well that should liven thing's up. Jack was ever the life of the party!"

THE MORNING two days after his arrival at Seven Oaks, Jack went to the armoury — a room displaying the weapons and armour of five generations of Elliot's. It was his favourite room in the house. As boys he and Denzil had haunted the place, weaving stories about their illustrious ancestors from the items on display and playing knights and brigands with their wooden swords and shields. As they grew older and were permitted to handle the treasures on the walls and in the cabinets, they learned the skills of swordsmanship and shooting, trying the various weapons out for fun and practice. He was the more accurate marksman, but Denzil, being lighter on his feet, was the better swordsman.

Jack wandered around the room reacquainting himself with old friends. The room was situated in the oldest part of the house and went back to the 1640s. It was almost square with a high domed roof and huge fireplace that took up most of the wall opposite the doorway. Mullioned windows were let into the wall on the right and the wall opposite was covered floor to ceiling with cabinets storing the various armaments of past scions of the house of Elliot. Above the fireplace a pair of crossed swords were displayed below a shield bearing the coat of arms of the noble house.

The room smelt of polish and gunpowder and the smell brought back vivid memories. Jack went to one of the cabinets and took out one of the duelling blades and tested its balance. It was a sabre, heavy and wickedly sharp, even though it hadn't been tended to in a while. He sucked his thumb where the blade had sliced it like a paper cut. Smiling he tried the weight and balance of it, sweeping it through the air and trying a few lunges. The suit of armour in the corner observed his movements enigmatically and for fun he played at jabbing and slicing an imaginary opponent.

"Do you want to try a bout?" said a voice from behind him and Jack turned to find Denzil and Viviana standing in the doorway.

"Certainly, if you like. I warn you I've been practising" said Jack with a smile at Viviana.

She smiled in return and Denzil said "Oh, have you? Am I on my metal little brother?"

This was a joke, for Jack was the taller of the two, albeit by not much more than an inch or two.

Jack put the lethal sabre away and took out a pair of duelling foils from the cabinet. He checked the tips were in place on the foils and offered Den the choice of blade. Denzil took one and the two limbered up with the blades while Viviana seated herself in the window embrasure to watch them. Jack was conscious of her gaze as he tried to pretend that he wasn't.

They assumed the position, saluted, and began. Jack blocked Viviana out of his peripheral vision, focusing tightly on his opponent. He had been practising, but was it enough to beat Den in front of his lady?

They beat and blocked, each seeking an opening, a weakness in the others guard. Den was light and fast, Jack had greater reach and fractionally more strength. They were well-matched and Jack sought in vain for that opening. Each time he thrust, his brother's blade was there to sheer his away. He feinted high and went in low, but Den blocked and turned him aside again and again. Beat and beat and beat. They danced around each other, breath coming harder, sweat blooming on skin and soaking through shirts. Wrists turned and beat and sought and failed to find. Feet thumped on the floorboards, counterpointed by grunts of effort.

Jack pushed harder, he wanted to win this bout, suddenly it seemed very important. Unchivalrous as it was to show Den up in front of his betrothed. But Denzil was good, had always been good and Jack found himself on the back foot scrambling away from his brother's suddenly ferocious attack. Sweat ran into his eyes and his breathing became ragged. He was tiring. He suddenly dropped, Den's blade went wide, and he thrust up pinking his brother delicately over the heart. Den fell back with a panting laugh, and they disengaged.

Viviana applauded lightly and Denzil turned to her. "I am shamed my dear." Turning back, he said, "Jack you fiend, where did you learn that trick?"

"Too much free time in the barracks Den! I warned you I had been practising." Jack rested the swords on the side table and wiped his forehead with his sleeve.

One of the footmen appeared at the door. "My Lord, Mr Craig has arrived. Do you want him to come back later?"

Denzil groaned. "I had forgotten he wished to see me. No don't send the poor fellow away, I'll come." He turned to Viviana "My dear, duty calls can I leave you with Jack?"

"Of course, Denzil." They exchanged a smile that made Jack look away, acutely uncomfortable.

"I will see you at noon my dear. There is a matter of the tenants thatching I need to attend to. My Agent has been at me about it for some time and I keep putting him off." He kissed her cheek and left the room.

Jack had taken up a cloth and begun to polish one of the foils. Viviana began to wander round the room eyeing the various exhibits. She stopped in front of the suit of armour. She was a tall girl, but the armour was a full six feet in height and clearly made for a man of significant girth. "Who was this?"

"My great-grandfather, the 2nd Earl. He was a giant by all "accounts."

"Did they wear armour then? I thought it was only worn in the medieval period?"

"Apparently old Ralph was an antiquarian. He was obsessed with the knights of old and had the suit made up. The family folklore says that he had a quintain set up for himself and he spent hours practising. He kept trying to get people to joust with him but no one would do it. Drove my great-grandmama up the wall. Or more pointedly into the arms of Lord Rising."

"No!" said Viviana looking round at him. He put down the polishing cloth, laying down the foil carefully.

"Shockingly ramshackle my ancestors, don't let Den fool you they were all respectable. Do you want to see them?"

"What, your ancestors?"

"Yes, if Den hasn't shown you already? The gallery is through there." He nodded at a second door, between the cabinets. He held the door for her, and they passed out into the gallery which ran along the west wall of the house overlooking the gardens. Long stretches of wall interspersed with tall narrow windows, displayed a series of large portraits.

Jack led her slowly down the gallery telling her the stories attached to each, and she laughed at his comical tales and frowned over the sad ones. He watched the animation in her face and thought how beautiful she was. He had seen several beauties, and kissed his share of women, but this one... He dragged his eyes away and cleared his throat as they stopped in front of Earl Ralph.

"Oh my!" said Viviana eyeing Ralph's magnificence. "He was huge, wasn't he?"

"Yes, I feel sorry for his horse" remarked Jack.

She giggled and looked at the oval portrait of a woman's head displayed beside him. "Is that his wife?"

"The notorious Isabella." The lady was striking rather than

beautiful, but there was a martial light in her eye "Her affairs were legendary. Supposedly Ralph caught her in bed with one of her lovers, and it gave him an apoplexy. He died three months later. He was twenty years older than her."

"How sad," said Viviana.

"Yes, I think it was. They were clearly ill-suited. But I dare say the age gap was too much to bridge."

"What happened to her?"

"She broke her neck in a riding accident. Left four children orphaned."

Viviana flinched, or he thought she did, but the moment was fleeting as they turned and began to walk back. Jack, who was walking with his hands behind him, to avoid touching her accidentally on purpose, said, "How long have you known Den?"

She dragged her eyes away from Sebastian Elliot, the 3rd Earls younger brother, who bore an uncanny resemblance to Jack and said lightly, "Oh forever it feels like! He really only began to pay me attention in the little season. Let me think." She tapped her teeth with a neatly manicured nail. "It was the Castlereagh's ball, I think. We were seated together at dinner and I said something, I forget what, no doubt it was outrageous, anyway it made him laugh and really notice me. I think up 'til then he was just being polite." She gave him a sideways look. "Denzil is *very* polite!"

"Yes, I always called him sober sides."

She grinned showing her perfect white teeth, her eyes sparkled and his breath caught in his throat, *God and the Devil she was beautiful!*

"I thought he was very dull until…." She trailed off and coloured slightly.

"Until…" he prompted his eyes on her lower lip.

"Oh, I shouldn't say," she said, pausing in front a family portrait showing a man standing beside a seated woman, with a baby on her lap. Flanking him was a young boy with brown hair and on her other side a younger lad with fair hair. Seated at her feet was a girl. He stopped beside her wondering what precisely his brother had done to convince Miss Torrington that he wasn't a dull dog. "Is this you?" she asked pointing at the blond boy.

He nodded "Yes, I was about six when that was done and Den is twelve. Mary is eight. There is six years between me and Henrietta."

"My parents were a very unfashionable love match," he added, with a smile that made her blush and laugh.

"I can see that from the way she is looking up at him and the way their hands are clasped on her shoulder. Very unfashionable touches of intimacy," she remarked in a voice that sounded slightly strained to his sensitive attention. He realised with a jolt that his senses where she was concerned had become acute. "When did Den come into the title?" she asked.

"Five years ago. We lost mama two years before and Papa never recovered from her death. He just gave up. He was the most robust, healthy man you could meet. But Mama contracted some sort of wasting sickness. She was beginning to ail when Mary had her come out ball in the Spring of 1806. Watching her slowly die took the stuffing out of him. When she finally passed away, he just stopped. It took two years for his body to give up, but I think his soul followed her into the family vault."

He glanced down at her face, but it was turned away, he touched her shoulder lightly about to ask if she was all right. She shook off his touch with a shrug, and said in a voice gone husky with some kind of emotion, "And the baby, Henrietta? What happened to her?"

"We lost her to smallpox when she was five," he said, remembering a laughing little blond-haired angel whose passing had torn a hole in all their hearts, but especially his. Being closest in age he had taken the role of her protector as Den had taken Mary. He swallowed against a sudden lump in his throat.

"I'm sorry," she murmured, her eyes fixed on the portrait with a melancholy expression, which made him wonder when she had lost her parents and if there had been any siblings. He wanted to ask, but something remote in her face made him hesitate.

Lady Hartley appeared in the doorway. "There you are Viviana! Mrs Applegate was asking for you and I hadn't a clue where you were." She fluttered a handkerchief and smiled at Jack. "Captain!"

He bowed and smiled in return, squashing the surge of irritation at having his tete a tete with Viviana cut short.

Viviana smiled at him, but it didn't quite dislodge the sadness in her eyes. "I had best go, Mrs Applegate wants to show me the linen press." She turned and joined her grandmother at the doors at the end of the gallery that led to the main part of the house. He watched her go, wondering what he had stirred up. There was more to Miss Torrington than showed on the surface, he was sure of it.

CHAPTER 4

*M*ore and more people would begin arriving as Christmas approached, Denzil explained to Viviana. Christmases at Seven Oaks were first and foremost family affairs. But in addition to cousins, aunts, uncles and various distant connections, who all descended on the house for the festive season; various friends and acquaintance were also invited to leaven the potential powder keg of too many relations in close proximity.

A ball was being planned to be held two days before Christmas and Lady Mary drew Viviana into the preparations, much to Lady Hartley's delight. As she explained to Viviana it was an opportunity for her to learn her new role of Chatelaine to this vast pile of a house with its dozens of servants. Viviana did her best to take an interest in the domestic arrangements of the guests, and the merits of duck terrine over chicken pate as an appetiser.

She would have preferred to discuss the management of the Estate with Denzil. But when she tried to draw him out on the subject of tenants and farming, he told her she needn't both her head with such thing's. Conversely when she asked him his opinion of the decorations for the ballroom, he told her that he trusted her judgement in the matter.

~

THREE DAYS LATER, Viviana sat at the desk in the window embrasure the parlour, struggling with the seating arrangements for the ball, Lady Hartley snoring softly in a chair behind her, when Jack wandered in. Looking up with relief she said, "Oh Jack how timely! Please will you help me with this! Denzil is of no use whatsoever. I don't know who half these people are and I am terrified of placing someone in the wrong spot and bruising their consequence!"

Jack smiled and came over to her elbow, peering at her diagram and list of names. "You terrified of anything? I find that hard to believe," he said pulling up a chair. "Here let me look." He took the list and began to sort it. In a few minutes he had placed everyone. "That should do. Although I have some qualms about placing young cousin Algernon next to Great Aunt Matty."

"Thank you!" she said with a smile "How may I repay you?"

"Come for a walk with me. I see there is a break in the clouds. Heaven knows how long it will last, but I feel compelled to take advantage of it."

"Oh yes please. I would like it of all things. At least -" she glanced over at her grandmother, who had continued to sleep through their colloquy. The old lady chose this moment to wake with a start and sit up.

"Captain! Are keeping my granddaughter company?"

"Ma'am, we have just been sorting out the seating arrangements for the ball."

"The captain has just asked me to go for walk around the grounds Grandmama, you don't mind, do you?"

"But Viviana, the weather!"

"The sun is out, please say I may, I am dying for some fresh air!"

"I don't see why not, if you take your maid with you. You will have a care for her Captain?"

"I will," he smiled.

"Thank you, Grandmama!" Viviana kissed her cheek and flitted to the door. "Stay a moment Captain, while I put on my cloak and change my footwear."

He looked down at her slippers. "Yes, the ground is likely to be muddy, those wouldn't do at all."

"At least you don't think I will dissolve for a bit of mud! Denzil is convinced that no young lady could bear to get her feet wet indulging in anything so strenuous as a good tramp across the countryside."

SHE JOINED him shortly with a heavy cloak over her morning gown and spencer, and a pair of sturdy boots on her feet. Without her maid. When the Captain questioned her absence, she said, "Maria doesn't like walking and would slow us down. I can tell you are just as eager for a good brisk walk as I am."

"True," he said with a grin.

"What grandmama doesn't know won't hurt her," she said with a conspiratorial smile.

They set out across the open lawn towards the fields. The sun was doing its best to shine weakly through the break in the clouds and turn the soggy prospect, from grey and mud, to sparkling wet greenery. The air was crisp and cold and an occasional flurry of wind disturbed her skirts and at one point blew the hood of her cloak off her head and caused her hair to fly round her face.

Patting it back into order she laughed with the exhilaration of it and strode out boldly beside Jack, who was setting a cracking pace for them over the muddy, slushy ground. They'd had some snow overnight, but it had mostly melted, although there were occasional little piles of white dotted about in hollows or up against the surfaces of fence posts, trees, and the walls of buildings. They passed the stables and the barns and moved out into the open expanse of fields. They walked in companionable silence, each seeming to enjoy their own thoughts and the freedom to exert themselves in the outdoors.

They reached a fence and Jack helped her over the style, lifting her clear on the other side with his hands about her waist. For a second or two she was airborne in his arms and the feeling as he swung her round and deposited her on the ground was delicious.

She would have had to be made of stone not to notice how attractive her fiancées brother was, with his tall broad-shouldered physique and handsome open face with eyes that laughed. Yes, she decided glancing at him sideways, it was the way his eyes laughed, and caught hers across the room to share a secret jest between the two of them, that was so entrancing. She felt as if she had known Jack for ever. They had gone from strangers to friends in nothing flat. It was most disconcerting. She couldn't recall having ever met a gentleman she felt more comfortable with.

They reached another fence, and stopped to look at the grazing cows, which had been let out to find feed while the weather was clement enough. Leaning on the fence beside him, she said, "tell me about the War in the Peninsular. What was it like?"

"Uncomfortable mostly," he replied with an ironic smile.

"No, what is it like in the thick of battle?"

"Oh that." He stopped, staring across at the cows, as if he wasn't really seeing them. "Bloody uncomfortable."

She laughed because he was clearly intending to make a joke of it but persisted. "No, seriously I want to know."

"Why?" he asked scanning her face with those eyes, that weren't laughing now.

"Because," she raised and dropped a hand on the fence in a helpless gesture. "Because," she tried again. "I want to know what it is like to face death."

"Ah." He gazed at the cows again, while she watched his profile as he took out his thoughts and looked at them. "Well at the time, it is mostly like it's happening to someone else. But at the same time, you've never been more alive, precisely because in the next moment you could be dead. Before, you're nervous and trying to believe you'll see the other side of it. Afterwards, afterwards it's like you feel everything you couldn't during the battle. You feel all the aches and pains and horror and exhilaration. There's sadness and regret, for all the waste of life, and sometimes there's a kind of remorse for being one of the lucky ones. But there is the joy of being among the living too."

She nodded. "Go on."

He smiled at her briefly and went back to the cows. "It's deafening as a rule, what with the cries of the men and the cannon fire. And the smell can be suffocating, blood and mud, vomit and entrails, dung from horses and the scent of fear on the men, smoke from the canon. Sometimes a madness can seize you and that's when you're most out of your body, least aware of the discomforts and more hyper alert than if you've swallowed a gallon of coffee." He put a booted foot on the bottom rung of the fence. "But those moments are the shortest lived, although they don't feel like it at the time. For the most part, the army is dirty and damp, with uncomfortable barracks full of farting men, boiled cabbage and onions. Oh, and don't forget the paperwork; reams of it."

"But you love it?"

"It's all I know. I'm a younger son. I have to make my own way in the world. Not that Den would see me destitute, but I've no land or inheritance. Generally, it's the army or the church for men like me, and I'm not fitted for a religious vocation."

She tried to suppress a giggle at the notion of him in holy

orders and failed. They both laughed and of one accord turned and began to head back toward the house. As they went, he told her some tales of his experiences, generally ones that were funny. She stumbled at one point and his hand shot out to save her, clamping her briefly to his side until she got her feet under her. His hand was big and warm and his arm an iron band of reliable strength. She felt herself flush and bent over in a pretext of checking her boot to cover it.

They reached the house just as the clouds, which had been louring for some time, began to open and a heavy downpour commenced. Running at the last, they made it breathlessly to cover, a few damp patches on their clothing.

Standing in the vestibule of the side entrance to the house she laughed up at him "Thank you that was wonderful. I may now be able to support the tedium of the remainder of the day."

He seemed about to say something and changed his mind. He gave her a punctilious bow. "You are most welcome." He left her there, going through the side door towards the front of the house, and she took the back stairs to her bedchamber to change.

DESCENDING from her room having changed her boots and gown, the one she had gone walking in having got damp and muddy at the hem, Viviana sought Denzil and found him as usual in the study. He was seated at the large desk surrounded by papers, a robust fire in the grate keeping the chill at bay.

Pausing in the doorway she said, "May I come in?"

He looked up and smiled "Of course. You are a welcome distraction, I'm tired of accounts." He rose and came round the desk to meet her.

"What have you been doing?" he asked taking her in his arms.

She put her arms round his neck and offered her face for a kiss which he gave with enthusiasm. When she could speak, she said. "Trying to sort out the seating arrangements for the pre-ball dinner and failing abysmally. Fortunately, Jack rescued me. So, you may blame him if it doesn't work."

He led her to the settee in the room, and they sat, his arm round her and her head on his shoulder. "Oh, Jack will have got it right, he has a talent for diplomacy. It's why he was appointed to Castlereagh's staff."

She looked up at him. "I really like Jack."

He smiled. "Have you fallen for his charm? He is the best of good fellows. With the house filling up you will see him come into his own. He is much better at playing host than I am." He touched her face, turning her chin up so that he could kiss her again and she let him, evaluating the experience. His kisses were practiced, as polished as everything about him. With her eyes closed she wondered what Jack's kisses would be like. The thought, born out of nowhere, shocked her and made her pull back involuntarily.

Denzil looked down at her with a heated gaze and said apologetically. "I'm sorry my dear, you are so beautiful I get carried away."

With her heart thudding suddenly out of control she reached for him, anxious to blot out thoughts of Jack and kissed him with a fervour that elicited a response that shed polish in favour of passion. She was reminded of the kisses he had given her upon the occasion of their engagement and tried to lose herself in them.

"My dearest you will undo me," he murmured against her hair. She could feel his heart thudding under her hand and took a breath to steady her own breathing, realising that he would interpret her agitation as desire for him. Which was true up to a point. She wasn't indifferent to him, but she was aware of a Jack shaped shadow between them. She gave an internal shake to banish it, and said softly, "Denzil."

"Yes, my darling?" he asked, gazing at her with such adoration that her heart contracted, and she felt suffocated.

She withdrew gently from his embrace and he let her. She rose and he followed automatically. She said awkwardly, "I should find Mary, she wanted to go over the arrangements for the ball." It was an excuse, but he accepted it easily, kissing her hand by way of letting her go. She went to the door, glanced back to see him watching her with that same look of drunken adoration, and she escaped with a thumping heart and a fluttery panicked feeling in her stomach.

OUT IN THE hall she paused wondering whether she should retreat to her room and deciding against it. She crossed the hall to the back parlour and found Mary, Wroxton and Jack, grandmama was having a lie down. Mary was engaged in some embroidery, Wroxton had the paper over his face and was snoring gently, his feet stretched out to the fire and Jack was seated before a chess board frowning.

Mary looked up from her tambour frame and smiled and Viviana returned the smile, but she gravitated towards Jack involuntarily. "What are you doing?"

"Playing against myself" he admitted with a rueful smile.

"And who is winning?"

"He is," said Jack with a nod at the opposite side of the board.

"Will you play against me?"

"Can you play?"

"Of course. My great Uncle Vincent taught me," she said taking a seat opposite him.

He re-laid the board and offered her white. She opened boldly with Queens knight to Rook four, and he threw her a look of speculation. She always played bold. It sometimes came back to bite her, but frequently worked in her favour, disconcerting her opponent. He made a conventional opening, and they played turnabout in silence to the backdrop of Wroxton's gentle snores and the crackle of the fire.

She contemplated the board, trying to see several moves ahead. She made her decision and moved. Then sat back with satisfaction, stretching out her slippered foot under the table and encountered his boot. His eyes flickered to hers and then back to the board, and she felt herself flush with a sudden awareness. Yet she didn't move her foot and neither did he. Her heart accelerated in acknowledgement of that. She bit her lip and watched his hand, with strong slender fingers and square capable palm, reach out and take one of her Bishops. She smiled she had anticipated this. She moved her Queen. "Check."

She watched him, waiting for him to interpose his Knight. It was the obvious move. He licked his lower his lip, and she played with the gold locket she wore round her neck, her slipper still pressed against his boot. He glanced at her again, but his eyes were on her hand where it rested on her décolletage fiddling with the gold chain of her filigree locket. She suddenly remembered to breathe, which expanded her rib cage and made her breasts rise under her hand. His eyes dropped to the board again, and she let out her breath silently, waiting, her heart beating more rapidly. After an endless moment, he moved his Bishop instead, threatening her Queen and forcing her to retreat.

She shrugged and with a wry smile complied. She had retreated but did not intend to do so for long. If he made the move she expected, he would make next, she would checkmate him in three moves.

Instead, he moved a rook. She frowned, contemplating this strange tactic. She dropped the locket, and it nestled into her cleavage while she leaned forward on her elbows. She felt him move back in her peripheral vision, his boot pressed harder against her foot as he shifted in his chair. She moved her Queen, lining up on the knight and beyond it his King. His hand rested on the table by the board and his fingers tapped absently.

She resisted the urge to edge her hand out towards his, instead clasping hers together in front of her breasts. She watched his face raptly and saw the covert glance he threw at her hands. He moved a pawn threatening her Queen. Suddenly she saw what he was doing. He had pinned her Queen on three angles, forcing her to move into a place that took his King out of immediate danger. She made the move, she had little choice. But she extended the move across three spaces and by doing so regained the potential to get him into check again in the next move. He smiled, and she tried to decide if he saw what she saw. He rubbed his upper lip with his knuckle and moved that rook again. She moved her Queen and spoke softly. "Check," at the same time, she moved her slippered foot along the side of his boot. "Do you concede?"

He sat very still for a moment, pointedly not looking at her. Then withdrew his foot. After a moment he picked up his king and laid it down, conceding her the game. She ought to feel pleased, but the withdrawal of his foot, shocked her into the realisation of what she had been doing, and she flushed, pushing her chair back and was about to rise when the door opened and Denzil came in.

CHAPTER 5

 s the house filled to bursting point with people, Denzil had cause to be grateful for his brother's presence. It was his duty as Lord of the demesne to greet and speak with each of his guests, and he did it cheerfully enough, but it was still a strain. One he was glad enough to eschew in favour of a quiet hour in the study. Whereas, watching Jack moving effortlessly among their guests, sharing a jest, paying a compliment, introducing strangers to each other and steering enemies away, he knew a moment of envy. Jack's poise and diplomatic skills had clearly been honed to a fine point since he was home last. All those months of doing the pretty among the generals in Vienna had paid off. But Denzil knew it was more than that. Jack had a naturally more outgoing nature than his own. That which was a strain for him, came easily to Jack.

He noticed too, looking round the ballroom that Viviana had little trouble mingling with the guests. True she was more popular with the gentlemen than the ladies, but that was perhaps to be expected. Her hand was solicited for every dance. Fortunately for the look of things, she had reserved two dances for him and of course he escorted her into dinner. It had been a year since this ballroom had been used. He was not in the habit of entertaining, but he supposed that would change now that he was to be married.

Watching Viviana tread the lively steps of the cotillion, he thought with satisfaction how lovely she was and, yet again, how lucky he was to have secured her hand. They would of course entertain a great deal more, but with the setting up of the nursery, the pace would no doubt abate and bit, and he could spend a larger amount of his time here at Seven Oakes. He certainly preferred the life of a country gentleman to that of town beau and was looking forward to the natural progression of life that would bring that about.

Viviana was laughing at something her partner said, and he was struck again by the milky smoothness of her white skin, the glossy black of her hair and the vividness of her blue eyes and rose lips, enhanced no doubt by a little rouge. Would she bequeath those beautiful features to their children?

Someone nudged his elbow and his brother murmured in his ear, "You're neglecting your duties Den." Jack handed him a champagne glass which he took absently and sipped.

"You're right I am."

"Lost in admiration of your lady?"

"Right again. I'm the luckiest dog, Jack, I still can't quite believe it."

"You will have to liven up a bit sober sides. The lady requires entertaining," remarked Jack, taking a generous swallow of his champagne.

"Oh, initially I daresay, but once we have children no doubt she will settle down" responded Denzil equably.

JACK CHOKED and turned it into a cough. "No doubt," wheezed Jack as Denzil slapped him on the back helpfully. "At least," he said having caught his breath "your children will be beautiful."

"Yes, I was just thinking that myself," said Denzil and wandered away leaving Jack to stare after him with a frown between his brows.

The subject of their discussion chose that moment to flow off the dance floor and arrive at his elbow in a sea of white lace and satin, towing her red-faced partner and demanding champagne. The red-faced man, whom Jack recognised as the local squire, retired to the safer realms of his wife's plump petticoats, and Jack provided the requested champagne.

"Enjoying yourself?" he asked.

"Oh yes, are you not?" she replied breathlessly fanning herself. "Gosh, it's hot in here!"

"Come this way," said Jack leading her to an alcove that gave onto a little balcony accessible through a set of French windows. They stood outside, sheltered from the weather by a generous balcony above, and she sipped her champagne and sniffed great lungful's of cold air. The low-cut gown allowed a delightful view of her white bosom while she did this, and Jack took shameless advantage, leaning against the wrought iron railing of the balcony. The night was semi clear, a few clouds scudded across a half-cut moon. The air was cold and bracing.

"Better?" he enquired.

"Yes. Much! What were you talking to Denzil about? He wandered off before I could join you."

"He was admiring your manifold charms, and I was agreeing with him," said Jack, lazy with champagne and the intoxication of her presence.

"Did you?" she asked, and he rather thought she flushed, though it was difficult to tell in the light.

"Yes, he was saying how much he looked forward to setting up the nursery!" said Jack with a laugh in his voice.

She stiffened slightly and waved her fan, partially covering her face. "Did he?" her voice sounded peculiar, and he narrowed his eyes, focusing on what he could see of her face.

"That is hardly a proper topic for conversation, is it?" she responded.

"Oh, I don't know. He would be delighted with a son in your image no doubt, as should we all, despite the fact that the sprog will cut me out of the succession," remarked Jack teasingly.

She rallied at his tone. "You could hardly expect to succeed Denzil, there is, what, six years between you?"

"Just under," he admitted. "He was born in August, and I was born in May, with Mary between us. And no. I don't expect or wish to succeed him. I will be very happy to dandle my nephews and nieces on my knee."

"Would you not prefer your own Jack?"

He finished his champagne and said coolly, "In good time. The soldier's life leaves no place for a wife and family."

"You left no girl broken-hearted in Spain?" she asked twiddling with her champagne glass.

"No and not in Vienna either."

"I don't think I believe you Jack. They may not have broken *your* heart, but how can you know there wasn't some poor soul eating her heart out for you?"

"I did nothing to cause any woman to form an attachment to me," he responded. The moon had gone behind a cloud and his face was in shadow.

"You hardly need to do anything to make a woman fall in love with you Jack." Her voice was so low he was about to ask her to repeat what she had said when the sense of her words burst in on him. In the next breath she said, "I am getting cold, let's go back in."

He assented and held the door for her while she swept the generous skirts of her lace ruffled gown past his legs. In the ballroom he soon lost her to the importuning's of her next partner, and he wandered off to find another drink. His heart was beating much faster than it should be, considering he had not indulged in any exercise.

. . .

TWO DANCES LATER, Denzil secured his betrothed to himself and inveigled her into sitting the next number out with him in the cloakroom! This shocking turn of events came about because when he appeared at her elbow to lead her onto the floor, she looked up at him from her seat and said, "Oh Denzil, someone had trod on my lace and ripped it!"

He crouched to look at the damage and noted that indeed one of the flounces was ripped. "Do you have some pins?" he asked

"Yes, in my reticule"

"Come into the cloakroom, and I'll pin it up for you" he said practically.

She gave him her arm, and they walked discretely round the outside of the dance floor. They reached the door into the cloakroom and with a quick look round to check that no one was paying them any attention, he held the door open for her. She slipped inside, he followed closing the door and locking it cautiously. He had no wish to be caught redressing his fiancé.

He smiled to himself turning towards her. Not that this was too shocking, but by rights she should have had one of the women do it for her. As her betrothed, he had some rights and privileges, and he intended, on this occasion, to take advantage of them. Was it the champagne talking? That and the fact that he had barely had a moment alone with her in days.

She had taken out the pins and was examining the damage. He crouched at her feet and pinned up the torn flounce. It was the work of moments. "There" he said sitting back on is haunches, "No one will be able to tell without examining it closely."

She smiled down at him. "Thank you! I didn't know how useful you could be Denzil."

He rose easily and put his arms round her. "You can find another way to thank me if you like."

47

"Denzil are you disguised?" she asked with a mock shocked expression.

"Not above par you baggage. It's the champagne, and you! Enough to make any man lose his head!" he said, lowering his head to kiss her.

She turned her head, "it's hardly proper to be kissing me in the cloak room Den," she said.

"You're right, I am intoxicated." He said with a rueful smile. "Will you deny me even one kiss?"

She looked up at him, but he had the strangest sensation that she wasn't seeing him, but something or someone else. She shook her head and smiled. "Of course."

He bent his head and he kissed her, but he could feel a reserve in her response that hadn't been there before. He was about to deepen the kiss in an attempt to elicit a stronger response when a rattle of the door handle interrupted them. Flushing, he put his finger to his mouth to quiet her and they both held still until the intruder went away.

His hands still on her waist he let his fingers caress her through the fabric of her gown and murmured, "we should return to the ballroom before we are missed."

She nodded and stepped out of his embrace, turning to the mirror on the wall to check that her coiffure was undisturbed. Standing behind her and looking at her in the mirror, he said,

"What is it my dear?"

She flushed and shook her head. "Nothing!"

"It's not nothing when you pull away from me like that. You used to like my kisses."

"I do. You're a very good kisser Den."

"Then let me kiss you properly?" He turned her gently and lifted her chin to plant a soft kiss on her lips. His hand slipped around to hold the back of her head and his arm encircled her waist pulling her closer as he deepened the kiss. She remained stiff a moment longer in his embrace, and then she slid her hands up over his chest to link them behind his neck and pressed herself closer against him.

He released her mouth with a tender lingering kiss and said huskily, "My dear you set my blood racing."

She smiled at him and said softly, "You are a very good kisser Den."

"Is that accolade bestowed from your vast experience my dear?" he jested trying to lighten the mood.

Her eyes widened and she said, "How many men do you think I've kissed?"

"Like that? Not many, I hope. Preferably none at all" he responded quickly.

She flushed slowly, withdrawing her hands from round his neck. "And if I had?"

"You're funning I know," he said making a quick recover. "But you shouldn't joke about such things, at least not with anyone but me. They might get an odd idea of you."

"But you wouldn't get an odd idea of me?" she asked looking him in the eye with a gaze that told him she wasn't pleased.

"Of course not!" he said.

"Well, I am glad of that" she said. He still had his hands on her waist, but he felt her pulling away and let her go, the moment was spoilt, and he was cursing himself for his clumsy tongue. At the same time, he was disturbed in a way that he couldn't put into words. Her initial reluctance to let him kiss her, and now this prickly response to a mild joke?

"We should probably go back, we will be missed and that will cause gossip," he said offering her his arm.

She took it but tugged him round to face her. "I am a shocking flirt Denzil, but I am not a whore!"

He felt himself stiffen and flush. "Good God Viviana, I never said you were, nor did I think it! Please moderate your language. If anyone heard you -"

"Do I have to moderate my tongue with you?" she asked, her

eyes showing a brightness that made him feel wary. Was that anger or tears?

"Well only in public I suppose, but I would rather you didn't speak in that intemperate style!"

"We're not in public now!"

"You're splitting hairs!" he said exasperated.

She gasped and giggled suddenly.

"What?" he said still nettled.

"Why are we quarrelling over nothing?"

He let her smile tease one from him. "I don't know. I'm sorry darling, you may say whatever you like. I don't mean to be a –"

"Sober sides?" she prompted with a cheeky smile.

"You've been talking to Jack" he said taking her back into his arms.

She let him kiss her, her hands on his shoulders. With harmony restored between them, they returned to the ballroom. They had missed their dance, and he surrendered her to her next partner with a good grace.

But later, when retiring to bed, the episode came back to trouble him, and it was a while before he slept.

CHAPTER 6

*I*t was Christmas Eve and the company were engaged in a silly game of snap dragon. This delightful game was a tradition in the house for Christmas Eve. Bowls of flaming brandy filled with raisins were brought into the great hall, which was the setting for this game and placed upon each table round which clustered the contestants. All the lights were extinguished save the glow from the enormous fireplace at one end and the flaming bowls of liquor, which threw shadows on the assembled company. The game was played in two rounds, a winner being found for each table from the first round and then the winners would play off against each other in a second round.

Generally, only the gentlemen played this game, the ladies being afraid to dip their fingers in the flames. But Denzil being at a table with his fiancé, his sister and her husband, Ashley Morton, Georgiana Hennessy and her husband Franklin and his uncle Sir Percival Blount, discovered that both Viviana and Georgie were eager to play. Sir Percival and Mary sat out, but everyone else was game to try and much shrieking and merriment ensued as fingers dipped into the flambeaux and came out dripping with blue flames. It was a messy game and induced much hilarity in the participants.

Denzil, having succeeded in retrieving his third raisin was wiping his fingers on his handkerchief and watching his beloveds attempts to extract one of the slippery little devils from the flaming liquid, much encouraged by other members of the board. As her fingers scrabbled for the elusive fruit, Georgie likewise dipped for them. Both women succeeded in extracting a raisin each and Mary, who was keeping count, announced that Viviana was now in the lead.

"Denzil you are not going to let her win, are you?" exclaimed Mary.

"Certainly not!" he responded dipping again. All hands reached for the bowl and there was a mad scramble to find the remaining raisins. "Ha!" said Denzil extracting two at once and holding them up for the adjudicator to see.

Ashley found his first raisin and popped it in his mouth with lazy aplomb. Wroxton found his second and Georgie exclaimed, "Oh I have one! Oh, no!" as the slippery fruit slid away from her groping fingers.

Viviana extracted one and then another in quick succession, popping them into her mouth and wiping the run of brandy from her chin with her fingers and laughing with delight. Denzil watching her eyes sparkling and the brandy glistening on her lips, felt full up with love for her and longed to reach out and kiss her. That was impossible of course. She seemed oblivious of his stare, caught up in the game. He was too distracted to play properly and as a result she proved the winner of their table.

The winners from each table were gathered into one table for the play off. His brother was of course one of these and Denzil stood behind her chair while she played, strangely conscious of his brother seated beside her at the table. In the end Jack won of course, but Viviana was declared the runner-up. And when the flames were all extinguished and the only light was afforded by the fireplace, she rose a trifle unsteadily to her feet and allowed Denzil to catch her as she swayed slightly and murmured with a giggle, "I fear I may be a trifle disguised. Denzil are you cross with me?"

He was in fact but chose not to show it. The servants would soon have the candles relit. He used the momentary shadow to murmur in her ear, "My dear you should retire for the night."

"Nonsense!" She said, more loudly than he liked. "I am not the least bit tired! Don't spoil sport Denzil!"

"The brandy was a little strong my dear, and you are clearly not used to it. I shouldn't have let you play." He said quietly, drawing her out a side door and into an ante chamber, conscious of the other guests milling about and moving off for supper. The room was lit only by an oil lamp on the table, leaving the corners in shadow.

She laughed "And how would you propose to stop me?"

Her eyes glittered in the half light, her face was flushed, and she smelled of brandy. He was conscious of a wave of irritation with her wayward behaviour. She was embarrassing him, and it made him acutely uncomfortable. His tone was brusk.

"I must insist Viviana, that you retire. It would not be seemly for you remain in company in your current condition!"

She burst out laughing. "Denzil don't be so stuffy! I shall be perfectly recovered in a little while, and you may remain with me until the effects wear off." She moved towards him and put her arms round his neck. "Please! Don't send me to bed like a naughty child!"

"Viviana!"

She reached up and silenced him with a kiss.

The sound of a door opening and an incoherent "God I'm sorry –"

Made the lovers spring apart with guilty fright.

Jack stood on the threshold, the lamp light threw shadows over his face, but did not disguise his expression. Denzil was aware of flushing furiously, extremely embarrassed to be caught thus in a passionate embrace.

"Jack! Were you looking for me?"

"Yes, supper is about to be served, and you are required to make the Christmas Eve toasts."

"Of course." he looked down at Viviana who had her eyes lowered.

"Jack, Viviana has had a little too much brandy, will you remain with her until she is recovered?"

"Ah, yes of course." Jacks voice was husky which was odd.

"Viviana you will mind Jack and join me when you can comport yourself with requisite sobriety!" He nodded to them both and stalked from the room, more annoyed with his betrothed and himself than he could ever recall being before.

JACK STARED after his brother and then turned back to Viviana, who had collapsed in fits of giggles in the chair by the table.

"Stay there, I will fetch you some coffee," he said beating a hasty retreat.

He returned with two cups, the sugar bowl and a hot pot of coffee, which he set down on the table. Taking a seat, he poured them both a cup.

"Drink this!" He said pushing it towards her.

She rested her chin in one hand and stirred sugar into her coffee with the other. "He tried to order me to go to bed like a bad child!"

"That would probably be the best solution." He sipped the bitter black brew.

"Nonsense I shall be fine presently." she took a sip of coffee and set the cup down carefully in the saucer. "Is he always this stuffy?"

"You embarrassed him."

"That is evident." She stared into the cup and took another sip. "Would I have embarrassed you?"

"The situations are completely different. I'm a soldier. My wife will not be the Marchioness of Stanton."

She reached across the table and took his hand. "Your wife will be a very fortunate woman."

The spark ignited at her touch made him jerk his hand away. "I will fetch your grandmother, this is not seemly," he said rising.

"No, please don't! I'll be good I promise." her palpable distress, made him sit down again.

"Why do you do this?" he asked quietly.

"Behave badly?" she asked not misunderstanding him.

"You obviously know how to behave, yet you cannot resist flouting convention at every turn. Why?"

She shrugged. "They say I am too like my mother."

He was about to ask her another question when Lady Hartley appeared in the doorway.

"Viviana, Lord Stanton sent me to fetch you. Are you quite recovered? If not, you should retire -"

"I am perfectly well Grandmama," she said rising with stately dignity. "Thank you for the coffee, Jack," she nodded to him and accompanied her grandmother from the room.

Jack sat finishing his coffee in a brown study.

CHAPTER 7

wo days after Christmas, most of the guests had departed and the weather, which had been grey and dull and cold for days, suddenly offered sunshine which sent the remaining members of the party outside.

Assembled at the stables, Viviana discovered that her mare, Lady, had developed a limp. Mary said, "Oh you may have my mare if you like, I will stay here."

Viviana turned to her warmly. "On no account! I am sure Denzil can mount me. Surely you have a horse I can ride Denzil?" she said turning to him.

Straightening from examining Lady's foreleg he said, "Yes of course. I have two mares that you might find suitable. He led her down the aisle between the stalls pointing out the horses to her. They passed a stall in which a large black stallion was housed and Viviana exclaimed, "Oh what a magnificent fellow!" The horse was seventeen hands and beautifully shaped, with a glossy black coat and white blaze on his forehead. He kicked the stall truculently as they stood watching him.

"Yes, but a complete devil, he is called Tempest for that reason. Barely broke to bridle," responded Denzil passing him by, but Viviana stayed to coax him, offering an apple. He eyed it suspiciously, and she waited patiently for him to come to her. Denzil realising that she had not followed him, turned to watch her with the horse. She spoke softly to him, and eventually he approached and took the apple, even letting her stroke his nose for a bit before throwing his head with a snort and backing away.

She turned. "Do you ride him Denzil?"

"He's not mine. Belongs to Jack, vicious devil. I've stabled him the last two years while Jack was on the continent."

"Have you ridden him?"

"A few times. But I prefer a more obedient mount. He is hard work."

She grinned. "Oh yes he would be a challenge!" She turned her head and called, "Jack! Are you going to ride this magnificent animal?"

Jack who was leading Lady Mary's palfrey out of its stall turned his head and called "Not today. He can't be trusted to keep the line in company." He handed the palfrey over to the head groom and came towards her. "He has a devilish habit of nipping the flanks of other horses." He stopped by the stall and held out a hand to the creature. Tempest nickered in acknowledgement and reluctantly approached him. "I may take him out later to knock the fidgets out of him. He needs a good run daily or his disposition sours. Doesn't it, you spawn of Satan?" he said stroking the stallion's shoulder.

"You must show me his paces later," she said. "I would dearly love to ride him."

"Good heavens Viviana he is no ride for a lady," interposed Denzil. "He is wild to a fault!"

She raised an eyebrow. "Oh, I could handle him!"

"No, you could not! You remember I've ridden the creature. It took all my strength and skill to hold him. He would throw you in an instant."

"How much would you like to wager against the chance?" she challenged.

"Nothing. Don't be ridiculous. You will not ride him."

Her mouth set. "He is not your horse but Jacks! May I ride him, Jack?" she said turning the full force of her sparkling eyes on him.

Jack met his brothers fulminating glare over her head. "Denzil's right, Viviana. Tempest is no fit horse for a lady, no matter how skilled a rider."

"Oh, please Jack!" She wheedled, laying a hand on his arm. He looked down at her and shook his head.

"My brother has said no, Miss Torrington. It is not my place to overrule him in matters of your conduct."

"But if Denzil had not said no, you wouldn't be so obdurate, would you?" she narrowed her eyes at him and said softly, "I am sure you think I am equal to anything."

"What I think is immaterial. The answer is no Miss Torrington and there's an end of it." He turned and walked away, and she looked after him with a decided pout. She shook her head as if shaking off something unpleasant and turned back to Denzil with a sigh.

"Very well I shall be good. Show me this mare you have for me."

Denzil took her arm and lead her to a stall further down the row, trying not to feel both shocked and irritated by the little scene just enacted.

Viviana accepted the mare he offered with every show of complaisance and the riding party mounted up and left the stables for an enjoyable hack across the countryside.

THE NEXT MORNING Viviana rose early and commanded her maid to lay out her riding dress. "Yes Miss of course."

Viviana surveyed herself in this garment, which was one of her favourites, it being of dark sapphire blue velvet just the shade of her eyes and showing her figure to advantage, she said to her maid, "Now you are to say nothing of me going out do you hear? I am still abed with the headache. And should anyone ask to see me I am asleep. You understand?"

"Yes Miss, of course. But where are you going?"

"For a ride of course!" smiled Viviana, opening her door, and checking that the hallway was empty.

DENZIL ENTERED the breakfast parlour to find his brother addressing a large plate of bacon, beef and eggs. He was surprised to find no sign of Viviana. It was her habit to rise early and breakfast with him and Jack. He enquired and was told that Miss had the headache and was sleeping late. Denzil frowned and requested her maid to attend him.

This damsel entered the breakfast room with trepidation and bobbed a curtsy. A few questions elicited a whispered and awkward response, with a flushed and uncomfortable expression. Denzil concluded that his betrothed was suffering from a female malady and was secretly relieved at this first sign of feminine weakness. The maid slipped from the room and Jack emerged from the paper in which he had taken refuge during this whispered colloquy. "I fancy I will go for a ride this morning Den, can I tempt you to accompany me?"

Denzil cut into the beef. "I would love to Jack, but I have my Steward, Ferris coming to me this morning."

Jack drained his coffee cup and regarded his brother sympathetically over the rim. "The burdens of office!"

"Something like that."

"Well, I'll bid you good-morning." Dropping his napkin on the table he left the room and strode out to the stables. Entering he ran his eye along the stalls and immediately perceived that one was empty. He called to the groom who hurried in from his task of shoeing one of his lordship's greys.

"Yes, Master Jack what is it?"

"Where is Tempest?" asked Jack grimly.

"Why in his stall –" the groom stopped when it became obvious that the black stallion was not in his stall.

Jack frowned and said curtly, "Saddle Badon for me." He went back out into the yard looking at the marks on the ground. The warmth of the last couple of days had softened the ground a little and by dint of careful searching he thought he distinguished fresh hoof prints leading out of the yard and in the direction of the woods.

The groom led out his saddled and bridled horse, and he mounted the brown gelding, pulling Badon's head round he set off in the direction he thought she must have gone. He should of course have alerted Denzil, but he hoped that perhaps he could find her and bring her back and that Denzil need not know about this escapade. His thoughts were dark indeed as he brooded on his brothers betrothed.

In the space of a month, he had seen ample demonstration of the lady's spirit and her complete disregard for Denzil's wishes and feelings. She was a selfish, wilful baggage with the soul of a lightskirt. He could understand Denzil being dazzled by her, but a less suitable bride for his straight–laced, kind-hearted brother he could not have imagined. Well, she should be brought to reason and shown in no uncertain terms the error of her ways. Den was too good for her, but if he was bent on having her, damn it, Jack would see her schooled and fit to grace his brother's table.

It was a fresh clear morning and if he hadn't been so furious, he would have enjoyed the ride. He kept his eyes peeled as he urged his steed to a faster pace, thundering over the ground. He spotted her half an hour later, ahead of him. She had clearly taken the fidgets out of her restive mount for she was moving at a moderate pace, and he was forced to admit that she had an excellent seat.

Her blue gown hung over one side, a lovely contrast to the glossy black coat of the stallion. Just at that moment she turned her head, she must have heard him. She was too far away for him to see her expression, but she obviously recognised him because she raised her arm in a salute and then brought her crop down urging the horse to higher speed.

Jack watched with his heart in his mouth as the great beast reared and took off, careering away under a stand of trees, his rider clinging to his back as she vanished from sight beneath the branches. Without a second thought, Jack gave chase, tearing after her into the spinney. She was ahead of him, but he was closing the distance as she was forced to dodge among the trees and could not move so quickly.

He followed, taking a shortcut; he had the advantage of knowing the terrain better than she. He had played hide and go seek in these woods as a boy. He used the shortcut to come out in front of her and blocked her path as she came through the trees toward him. The stallion skidded and reared and for a moment he was sure she would be thrown. He reached out and grabbed the reign pulling the great beast down and to a standstill. Tempest didn't like this and neighed, tossing his head and tried to kick out with his legs. Jack manoeuvred his horse with his knees trying to keep him clear of the stallion's razor-sharp hooves.

The stallion was blowing, while Viviana was breathing hard her face flushed and shining with the thrill of the chase. "Oh, that was magnificent!"

"Do you have a death wish Miss Torrington?" he said forcing the stallion to hold still.

"Oh no! Just a love of excitement. And that was exciting you must own!"

"You are very fortunate not have broken your neck!"

"Oh nonsense! I told you I could handle him!" she said with a toss of her head. Tempest chose that moment for a show of restive temperament, kicking out with his front legs and Jack was forced to let go the reign or get his own mount kicked. With cool competence she brought the horse back under control. "There you see!"

"You disobeyed my brothers express order!"

"Yes, but only because it was silly!" she responded.

"Denzil has an exaggerated idea of my feminine weakness."

"Have you no regard for his wishes?"

"I should have, shouldn't I?" she shook her head "I told him I was too hot to handle."

"You are the devil's mistress Miss Torrington! Your selfish disregard for his feelings and your own safety are appalling! You deserve to be whipped!"

She flushed and stiffened in the saddle "Denzil would never do such a thing!"

"No, he is too much the gentleman! But I have less scruple's madam! I assure you it would give me great pleasure to whip you soundly. How dare you flout my brothers wishes and steal my horse without permission! Your manners are of the lowest order!"

Her hand came out and slapped his cheek. "How dare you speak to me that way!" Her eyes flashed with fury.

His cheek flamed under the slap, and he reached out and grabbed the riding crop dangling from her wrist. "You need a lesson, madam, in manners!" he said dismounting with a smooth movement. Before she could open her mouth to respond, he reached up and hauled her from the saddle and grabbing a strap from his own saddle dragged her over towards a tree. She screamed and kicked out struggling to get away from him.

"Stop it! Let me go! How dare you!" She panted trying to free his grip on her wrist. He shoved her against the tree and bound her hands round a branch above her head with the strap. She tugged at her bonds and screamed at him, "Let me go, you monster! Denzil will kill you for this!"

He shoved her back against the tree trunk fury thundering through his veins. Bare inches separated them, she gasped and her sweet breath, her scent got in his face. His body reacted to her closeness, her wild beauty, her flashing eyes, flushed cheeks and heaving bosom. She was desirable and dangerous. Which made him even more furious.

"No, he won't because you won't tell him." He spoke low and hoarse.

"Yes, I will!" she was panting with rage and frustration. "He will shoot a bullet through you and I will dance with joy! How dare you do this to me!"

"If someone had spanked you thoroughly as a child this wouldn't be necessary. Now listen to me! My brother loves you! God alone knows why, for a more spoilt, rag mannered termagant I've never met in my life! But I'm damned if I'll let you break his heart! Den is one of the best men to ever draw breath, and he wants you! So, by God you are going to behave yourself and treat him with the loving respect he deserves, or you'll answer to me! Do I make myself clear?"

"Ohh!" she screamed in impotent rage. "If I were a man, I'd put a bullet through you! In fact, if I had a gun, I'd do it right now! You beast! Let me go at once!"

"No, I will not!" He flipped her, so that her back was towards him, pressing her into the tree, with his hands on her slender waist, his nose full of the scent of her hair in face. He was out of his head with fury and something wild and untamed. "Clearly you do not understand anything but the rod! You seemed happy enough to use this crop on Tempest to force him to outrun Badon. Let's see how you like it!" With one hand in the middle of her back he swung the crop and laid it across her rump with a sharp thwack. Once. Twice. Three times he hit her with the crop, his arm shaking with anger and his body rigid with wild desire to bring her heel, for Denzil's sake. How dare she hurt him!

VIVIANA, pressed against the tree her wrists twisted in the strap, felt the crop land on her rump, but the impact was somewhat muted by the layers of her petticoats. She cried out with shock rather than pain. A rush of heat coursed through her body and took her breath away with each wack. Her heart thudded and skipped, her emotions a riotous mess of excitement, fear and fury. Never had she been treated so! His hand, hot in the middle of her back pressed her into the trunk of the tree, she plastered herself against it, her body flaming with a feeling she couldn't name.

His hand moved to her neck and she whimpered as his thumb caressed her nape, his fingers sliding across her shoulder. She heard the sharp intake of his breath and then an exhalation, that bordered on a groan. His hand dropped away leaving a cold shiver in the wake of the fire in his touch. He leaned in, his body crowding against hers, his voice soft and husky in her ear. "By what I hear you've had numerous offers, why did you accept Den's if you didn't love him? Do you care for him at all?"

Her breasts felt heavy and her nipples ached, she pressed them against the tree and struggled against the press of his body. An exasperated moan escaped her. "Of course, I do!"

Did she? Her body ached with a sudden longing she couldn't name. It made her arch against the tree and push her rump against him, where he pressed against her. He was hard and hot and oh God, her body trembled with a rush of tingling heat that made her knees go weak. For an endless moment neither of them moved. A thudding pulse beat in her throat and she closed her eyes as a wild impulse to turn and fling herself at this man who had dared to whack her with her own riding crop seized her.

In the next moment he moved away, cold air ran down her

back where his warmth had been, and she shivered, slumping in her bonds, only the straps keeping her on her feet.

"You have the strangest way of showing it!" His whispered his voice hoarse and aching.

Sharp longing made her eyes sting and she choked. "Oh, stop it!" Tears ran down her face and her head hung forward.

JACK STOOD BACK WATCHING HER, his chest heaving for breath, his body trembling, trying to bring his own wild reactions under control. He had never laid a finger on a woman, that he had raised the crop against her sickened him, and yet his impulse to go further than that, to turn her and possess her... Never had he felt such rage and liquid, ravening desire at once. This woman was so fucking dangerous and far too hot to handle. She would break Denzil's heart. Anguish and guilt cut through the drugging desire in his body. She belonged to Denzil. She wanted Denzil, not him. The wrongness of it screamed at him. He ignored it. Stuffed it down.

He shook his head to clear it and dropped the crop reaching to loosen the strap. Her arms fell limply to her sides and she turned slowly leaning against the tree. Tears stained her cheeks and her eyes were so dark they appeared almost black.

"I'm sorry," she whispered.

"Are you truly?" He asked keeping his distance, his body still pulsing with the residue of anger and desire. He ignored it. He had himself under control now, and it would never slip away from him again.

She swallowed. "Yes."

"Will you mind my brother's wishes in future?"

She looked down and then up and nodded, biting her lip.

"Then neither of us shall say anything further of this incident." the pulse in his throat skipped at the implied deception. He clenched his fists at his side.

"Which is more than I deserve," she admitted with a half-smile.

"Did I hurt you?" he asked abruptly. His heartbeat was still ragged. He swallowed, his throat dry.

She shook her head. "Not really, it was shock more than anything."

God, he was a beast! He stepped forward and took her hands examining her wrists, they were red where the straps had scraped her smooth white flesh. Guilt stabbed at him, and he rubbed them with his thumbs. "I'm sorry, I lost my temper."

"So did I," she admitted. He dropped her hands and turned back to the horses, scooping up her crop he held it, a memory of the fury that coursed through him when he wielded it against her swirling through him. How could he have done such a thing? What madness seized him? And how to stuff this genie back into its bottle?

"May I have it?" she asked, holding out her hand.

"Will you hit me with it?" he asked, trying for a lighter note to relieve the tension.

"I should," she responded following his lead. "But I am resolved to be good." She bowed her head a moment and then raised it saying softly. "Thank you. I think you may have saved me."

His heart thudded as he stared into her eyes. "From what?"

"Myself."

A SHOCK WASHED through his body as he saw what his brother might see to love in this unprincipled, immeasurably desirable woman. Her self-honesty was a kind of honourable courage. She was no self-deceiver. She knew what she was.

"If you show this side of yourself to Den, he will be your slave for life," he murmured, his hand coming up to cup her face.

She blinked tears from her eyes and for an endless moment he lost himself in their dark blue depths.

By sheer force of will he dropped his hand and turned away, his heart thudding, his body shaking with the effort to control the over mastering desire to pull her into his arms and kiss her.

She was his brother's fiancé. By dint of repeating that over and over, he was able to move away to the horses. Pretending to check the girth on Badon's saddle, he gave himself precious minutes to find composure. By the time he turned back she seemed to have done the same.

"I'm truly sorry for stealing your horse." true contrition sparked her voice. But then she ruined it with an imp of a smile venturing out. "But it was such fun, and I *can* control him!" she added defiantly.

He frowned at her in mock censure. "Perhaps, but you cannot go on just doing as you please with no regard for anyone else!" they must play out this farce, and they would each pretend the last few minutes had never happened.

She looked up at him ruefully. Or perhaps it was not a farce for her? She had not felt all that he had felt?

"You are perfectly right. The trouble is when the bit is between my teeth I don't think! I shall try to do better." Her eyes dropped a moment and she said softly, "I do *wish* that I was deserving of Denzil's adoration."

He lifted her chin with his fingers and surveyed her expression of sad contrition. "I do believe you are sincere. Strive to fulfil that wish and you *will* be deserving, Viviana."

She blushed and her eyes flooded with sudden tears. "I think that is perhaps the nicest thing anyone has ever said to me Jack. Thank you." She reached up and gave him a sisterly kiss on the cheek. The pressure of her lips, warm and soft on his cheek tingled and his body reacted again to her nearness. It took all his self-control not to seize her and-

She moved away towards the horses, saving him from himself.

Clearly whatever raging desires he was feeling she was not. Her affections were, if not firmly in Denzil's care, tending in that direction and who could doubt that she could and should love him, for Denzil was the best man he knew. This momentary lapse on his part should be, *must* be forgotten.

Both horses had ambled a little way off in search of grass. He followed her, catching the bridles. "We will return now, and I shall ride Tempest. And if you are fortunate, my brother will know nothing of your wickedness. He believes you currently to be still in bed nursing a sick headache."

"Yes, I know. I never get headaches," she said taking the saddle he removed from Tempests back while he swapped the one from Badon. He then lifted her saddle onto Badon's back, and they tightened the respective girths of their new mounts. He offered her his hands to assist her to mount and then mounted himself. They returned at a more leisurely pace to the house.

Just short of the house she dismounted and looking up at him said "Thank you for keeping my secret."

"Slip away to the back entrance. Hopefully no one will see you. Go!"

She went, he took both horses back to the stables and unsaddled and rubbed them down, attempting to banish the last hour from his mind.

CHAPTER 8

The following morning, after a restless night of guilt and self-recrimination, Viviana screwed up her courage and sought Denzil out in his study. He was writing when she came in, and she approached the desk with some trepidation. Her heart thudded in her chest and she felt slightly sick.

"Denzil, may I speak with you?"

"Of course, my love." he finished his sentence, put down his pen and rising, came round the desk.

"What is it my dear? Are you unwell still? You missed breakfast again."

"I am well. But I have a confession to make." she clutched her hands before her, biting her lip.

"Yes?" his voice was gentle.

Which made it worse. She took a deep breath and said quickly, "I took Tempest out yesterday for a ride."

"What?" He went white, his expression of gentle understanding evaporating, replaced by horror. "Are you mad? You could have broken you neck!"

"But I did not!" She said firing up.

"That is beside the point!" His breathing accelerated. His face closed but not before she glimpsed the hurt and disappointment in his eyes.

He paced away from her to the window where he kept his back towards her. "You disobeyed my direct order. Have you so little respect for my word?"

She looked at his back helplessly. "I'm sorry. I shouldn't have done it."

"No, you shouldn't."

"Can–can you forgive me?" She approached him tentatively.

He was silent so long she thought he wouldn't answer. He let out a breath on a sigh and her stomach dropped. She felt sick with guilt and self-loathing. He turned towards her and said quietly.

"I will, but not right now. Please leave me." His tone was cool and his expression remote. She shivered and bowed her head.

"Yes, my lord," she dropped a curtsy and left him.

DENZIL LISTENED to her steps walking away, his heart beating hard in his chest. He was shocked and an icy fury filled his veins. Disappointment warred with bewilderment. What could possess her to do such a thing? What had he got himself into? How could a young woman show such ill judgement, and so little regard for the proprieties? She was more of a child than he had realised. A revulsion of feeling washed through him. For the first time he seriously considered if he had made a mistake. All the doubts and niggles of the past month came rushing in on him, making him feel clammy and sick.

Leaving the study, he made his way to the stables where he checked the black stallion who appeared to have taken no hurt. Turning to the groom mucking out a stall he requested that his own mount be saddled. A few minutes later he left the stables setting his horse towards the tenant farms, pushing thoughts of Viviana from his mind. Even so it didn't relieve the burning anger, hurt and confusion in his chest.

By the time he returned to the house, the anger had burned to an ash and left a cold lump in his stomach. He went upstairs to change and returned to his study, requesting one of the footmen to send Miss Torrington to him.

VIVIANA RE-ENTERED the study vacillating between nerves and defiance.

"You wished to see me my lord?" she said coolly.

"Yes." He was standing in front of the fireplace, his hands behind his back. "I have had time to reflect on what you told me this morning, and it occurs to me that it is not only me that you owe an apology to, but my brother. Tempest is his horse. If you had met with a mishap the horse may have suffered a hurt as well."

She compressed her lips, her heart thudding loudly in her ears. She had attempted to keep Jack out of this, now he was determined to drag him in. "I have already apologised to Jack."

"Good. Was he angry?"

"Very," she said with emphasis.

He nodded. "I have had some time to reflect. I cannot pretend I am not hurt and disappointed with your wilfulness Viviana, nor can I profess to understand such reckless disregard for your own safety. But all that aside, I do acknowledge that you didn't have to tell me or Jack about it, since neither of us knew of it. The fact that you chose to confess, gives me hope that you have understood the graveness of your error and will not do something so heinous again. Am I right?"

"Please Denzil don't stand there all stiff and disapproving! I cannot bear it. I am truly sorry and will not disobey you again."

she said moving towards him. "Please forgive me?" She held out her hand.

He took it and kissed it. "Of course, my dear, if you are truly penitent."

"I am, I promise!" She flung herself into his arms and his closed round her. He kissed her hair, but she felt with a sinking heart that something was broken past mending. Jack's image danced behind her closed eyes. The feel of his body pressing her against the trunk of the tree would not go away. Her heart thudded and ached in her breast.

"Jack!" Viviana intercepted him on his way out the back door to the stables.

Pulling him into a side chamber she said quickly, "I just wanted to warn you that I confessed to Denzil about Tempest. He didn't take it well, but I didn't let on that you knew. So, he asked me to apologise to you too."

"Why did you do that?" His heart was thudding hard with alarm.

"I couldn't sleep!" she admitted. And it was true that she looked tired and wan, as if the events of the last few days had tired her more than he had realised. They had taken their toll on him too. She wasn't the only one who couldn't sleep. Although he doubted, she was tortured by the kinds of thoughts that kept him awake.

His heart softened at her expression of weary sadness. It seemed that she was indeed truly contrite.

"What did Den say?" he asked with sympathy.

"Oh, it wasn't what he said but the way he looked! So hurt and disappointed in me. I wanted to die a thousand deaths! It was awful! I'd much rather he spanked me like you did!" she confessed.

The surge of lust those words provoked made him move to the window, so she wouldn't see their effect on him. Standing with his back to her, he said as mildly as he was able, "I did warn you he would be hurt."

"Yes, it was excruciating."

So, she did care for Den's opinion then? His heart sank a little, but he shrugged it off. That was a good thing, she cared for him. He turned and found her closer than he'd realised.

"Thank you," she said with a watery smile.

"What for?"

"For being my friend. I–" she stopped and swallowed. "I don't deserve your forbearance, you could have told him what I did, and you didn't."

"I told you I wouldn't. I keep my word." he could never have divulged what happened between them to Den, it would be the worst betrayal of all. Den would never understand his assaulting her with the riding crop. For that alone Denzil would have called him out. Fortunately, Denzil wasn't privy to any of his other thoughts and feelings towards Miss Torrington either. If he ever so much as suspected... it would drive an irrevocable wedge between them. That was something Jack could not bear.

"I know." she smiled and squeezed his hand. He pulled his hand away and stepped back. He would have stepped around her towards the door but something that had been nagging at him, made him stop and ask. "When were you orphaned Viviana?"

She started at the abrupt question, coming as it seemed to out of nowhere. "Why do you ask?" her voice was husky and her eyes darkened.

"Because I am trying to understand you." The admission took him by surprise, but it was true. He was seeking a reason for her erratic behaviour. He wanted to understand her, to find an excuse for her behaviour.

"Papa died when I was twelve. Mama -" she stopped and swallowed. Then with a toss of her head that spoke volumes, she said, "Mama abandoned me at three."

"What do you mean, abandoned you?"

She laughed and the pain in it went straight through his chest. "She ran off with her lover and left me and papa. They told me she died." She stopped and swallowed. "On his deathbed, papa told me the truth. He said I was old enough to understand." Tears rolled down her cheeks and she wiped at them angrily.

"Her lover strangled her six months later and left her body in the rose garden. Papa found her, as he was meant to and spent the rest of his life looking for him, seeking vengeance."

"Did he find him?"

"Yes, he shot him. And suffered an apoplexy as a result." Her voice became suspended by tears. She gulped. "He died a month later."

"My God, I'm sorry Viviana." he put his arms round her instinctively and she rested her head against his chest briefly, but it seemed she couldn't remain still for she moved away. He ached to comfort her, but she didn't appear to want his comfort. He tried not to be hurt by that. It wasn't his place to comfort her. That was Denzil's role.

"I never speak of it." she wiped her face, sniffing. "Don't tell Denzil, please? The whole scandal was covered up. The story put about was that Mama became ill and retired to the country where she died. There were rumours apparently, but it was a short-lived wonder and the world moved on."

He nodded and swallowed. His throat was tight.

Lady Hartley's voice in the hall made Viviana start guiltily. "I must go, it wouldn't do for Grandmama to find me here." On the word she slipped out the door and left him prey to a wash of emotions.

He took them on his ride and returned to the house with a stronger determination than ever to avoid getting between Viviana and his brother. He hoped that she would feel able to tell

Den herself what she had confided to him. It made her behaviour so much more understandable. His heart ached for her. It was clear as day to him, that the pain of her mother's betrayal ran deep.

If Den understood that, he would love her fiercely and protect her with his soul. Jack knew that as well as he knew himself, for Den was the best of men. He deserved to be happy and sure he would be happy with Viviana once they got through these little teething spells. He swallowed the lump in his throat and went in search of Hardy. He desperately needed a bout of boxing to relieve the tension in his body and distract his over full heart.

VIVIANA FLED her interview with Jack and took refuge in her room. His question about her parents had raised emotions she normally kept firmly under lock and key. Her mother's betrayal was still raw. Anger and hurt warred with the creeping sense of her own unworthiness.

Denzil's hurt and disappointment scratched at her usual defences, undermining them. Would Den ever forgive her? She feared not. Tears seeped out from under her closed lashes. She had hoped that confessing to Den would make her feel better but in many ways she felt worse. His disapproval ate at her, and she found herself thinking of Jack.

She had been so angry with him for daring to tie her up and hit her with the riding crop. But if she was honest, it hadn't hurt more than her pride. If she was truly honest his anger, his passion had stirred a response she didn't fully understand or know what to do with. She had accepted Denzil's proposal because his kisses stirred her, made her feel some inkling of attraction. But Jack–

She sank back on her bed and stared at the canopy. The rush of heat, fury and excitement she had felt when he hit her with the riding crop had turned her bones to water. She had wanted to fling herself at him like the veriest trollop and beg him to kiss her.

Pride had held her back. And when he hadn't kissed her, she concluded that he didn't want to. That he was truly disgusted with her childish selfishness. Her heart cracked with shame.

She was like her mother, selfish, self-centred, a whore! She truly didn't deserve either of the Elliot brothers. A surge of self-loathing brought tears to her eyes, made her roll over and give into the tears she had been battling since Jack asked about her mother.

~

PEACE SEEMED to be restored for several more days. Viviana was a model of comportment and Denzil treated her with patient devotion. Guilt made Jack keep them both at arm's length and think seriously of leaving before his own ungovernable impulses lead him to do something he would deeply regret. She clearly was trying to make amends with Denzil, and he would not get in the way of that.

But it was also clear in under a week that the quiet life that so suited the Earl, Viviana found utterly boring. She tried to take an interest in the things the housekeeper told her. She tried to be supportive, and she tried very hard to be good. Within five days Jack could see her bursting to do something, anything, just for a lark.

No one could accuse Miss Torrington of being in anyway masculine, but Jack suspected she would have been much happier as a man. The restrictions placed upon a young unmarried woman were unbearable to one who obviously longed for freedom to express her vibrant spirit. His heart ached for her and his body itched with a longing that he steadfastly ignored; except in the privacy of his bed chamber where he took steps to relieve the tension but refused to indulge his imagination. During the day he avoided being alone with her and kept a firm lid on any stray memories of the incident beneath the tree. He had lost his mind temporarily, but no lasting damage had been done. Denzil's happiness was what mattered most.

To make it worse, the weather was so bad they were confined to the house, even riding was inadvisable. One evening they were all seated in the library, Lady Hartley had had retired to bed, and Lady Mary was yawning over her needlework, Wroxton having already left two days ago for London. Denzil was reading a book, Viviana was desultorily turning the pages of a women's magazine and Jack was perusing the Sporting News. Or at least he was trying to. He was altogether far too conscious of Miss Torrington's restless movements to concentrate. Finally, she threw the magazine aside. "Let me play you at Billiards! I cannot sit like this!"

Denzil buried in his book did not appear to have heard her. Jack looked at her over the Newspaper. "I'll play with you." He shouldn't, but he couldn't bear her restlessness.

She smiled gratefully. "Will you?"

"What was that my love?" asked Denzil looking up from his book.

"Don't bestir yourself Den. Viviana wants a game of billiards and I have agreed to oblige her."

"Watch out Jack! She is very good!" said Denzil with a fond smile, retiring into his book again.

They left the room and crossed the hall to the billiard room, leaving the door ajar as was proper. Jack set up the balls and handed her a cue, letting her break. The balls scattered and she sunk one.

They played turnabout, and Jack noted that she was very good indeed, unusual in a woman, billiards was not a female sport.

Examining the table intently she bent to sight along her cue and check the angle of a shot. It was one that required her to lie across half the length of the table. Watching her do this, Jack was forcibly reminded why this was not a feminine sport. The pose was three parts obscene and gave him a nice view of her rump. A gentleman, he reflected, would move, or at least avert his eyes. Jack concluded that he wasn't a gentleman. He should call an end to this and leave. He didn't.

His memories of thwacking that lovely bottom with the crop inevitably rising in his mind, causing other things to rise too. She stretched. Lined up the shot and putted. The ball rolled towards the pocket with a graceful slow-motion roll and went in. Straightening from the position almost sent her off balance, and he stepped forward instinctively to catch her. She fell back against him and froze.

He knew why. She could feel the evidence of his appreciation pressing firmly and warmly against that rump he had so lately been admiring. With the contact, his appreciation got firmer and warmer. All the memories and frustrations he had been fighting came flooding back in full force. His hands spread involuntarily over her stomach, pressing her closer, the rush of pure lust too strong to deny. Memories of pressing her against the tree, of her arching back against him, made him hard as iron. Her scent invaded his nostrils and his self-control snapped.

She dropped the cue, he had lost his moments earlier. She arched her neck in such obvious invitation, he kissed it before he realised what he was doing. He nuzzled the soft skin of her neck feeling her pulse and filling his nostrils with her scent. His lips on her neck, he had a perfect view down her generous cleavage and was in an equally perfect position to take in the import of her quickened breathing and suddenly taught nipples, pushing against the fabric of her gown.

God, she was as aroused as he was! As if to underline it, he caught the soft sound of an involuntary gasp in her throat and the raw flood of desire that unleashed, made him shudder and leak. He ached with wanting this woman. His hands clenched on her belly, and he felt her muscles contract under his fingers. He braced against her, clamping down on the urgent, overmastering desire to thrust against her. For a long moment he held her still, caught in the dizzying thought of lifting her skirt, bending her over on the table and ravishing her there and then. All the things he had steadfastly refused to let himself think about since the riding crop incident, flooded his mind in prurient, raw detail. His body flamed and he shook with ravening desire, shuddering with the fight for self-control.

A log fell out of the hearth and broke the spell. All the realities of their situation came crashing in on him, and he let her go, stepping away from her as if she were a branding iron. She turned in slow motion to face him, the horror he felt reflected back to him in her face. He willed her not to say anything. If they didn't speak of it, they could pretend it didn't happen. Like they had been pretending nothing had happened under the tree.

He bent and picked up the cues, placing them carefully on the table. "Goodnight, Miss Torrington." With a punctilious bow he left the room and walked on legs that felt like they didn't belong to him, up the stairs to his room.

He shut the door and leaned against it, staring with unseeing eyes at the canopy of the large four-poster bed that dominated the room. All the things he had been denying since the day she took out Tempest, and he tied her to a tree came flooding in. He had all but ravished the woman his brother loved. In his mind he'd already done it.

In his mind, in those long seconds while he held her frozen against him, he'd run his hands all over her luscious curves, squeezed her lovely breasts, caressed those beautifully pert nipples. He had moved his hand lower and cupped her sex, sliding his fingers between the slippery velvet lips between her parted legs. He was sure she would have been wet, even through the fabric of her gown! And lifted her skirt and had her over the side of the billiard table.

He leaked more fluid thinking about it; reliving the vivid

fantasy in every exquisite detail and twitching with involuntary raw desire, so sharp it was a physical ache, as fine and deadly as the blade of a rapier. He groaned aloud as his body shuddered and clenched, rigid with the desperate need for release. He sank to his knees and fumbled with the buttons of his breeches. Almost weeping with the intensity of it, he fisted himself rapidly, seeking an end to the ache in that frenzied stroking. It peaked in a matter of seconds, with an involuntary groan and flooded him in a few blessed moments of blinding, explosive pleasure, so sharp it bordered on pain.

Sobbing for breath with the relief, he sagged against the door behind him, his muscles gone limp, spasming randomly with the pulse of his heavily beating heart.

Sex was such a ridiculous act, he reflected with a weak laugh, imagining how absurd he must look. The back of his hand was wet with gobs of cooling fluid. A few spots lay on the carpet where they had landed. He got his feet under him and crossed the room to grab a towel from the dresser. Wiping himself down, he bent to scrub the spots from the carpet and sat heavily on the edge of the bed, staring at the cotton towel in his hands.

The thought of facing Denzil in the morning, of seeing her — no he couldn't do it. He would rather face Boney's charging army than that. He had to face the fact that he couldn't master this desire while the object of it was within his reach. Jack was no self-deceiver, and he realised that it was more than just nurturing inappropriately lecherous thoughts about his brothers intended. He could see her face, her eyes, as she stared back at him, the truth written in their depths. She was a beautiful, entrancing witch, and she would break Denzil before she was finished with him. He, Jack, could handle her, master her, Den never would. He swallowed. He couldn't stay and watch that.

He knew he loved her, perhaps she could or would love him. But she needed to discover that for herself and he wasn't going to wait around for her to find out. If there was any hope that her relationship with Denzil could work, he needed to clear out and leave them to it. If he stayed, they would never know, and he couldn't be the cause of Denzil's heartbreak.

The decision made, he reached for the bellpull to summon Hardy.

CHAPTER 9

*D*enzil entered the breakfast parlour the next morning surprised not to find his brother there before him. Helping himself to ham and eggs he had just sat down at the table when Porth entered with an envelope.

"My Lord, Master Jack left this for you. I understand he was called away in the night." The butler proffered the letter and waited clearly hopeful of being made privy to its contents. Denzil took the envelope with an absent thanks and broke it open spreading the single sheet out to read.

"He says that he has been recalled by his commanding officer to Geneva. The matter would appear to be urgent." As he raised his eyes, they fell on Viviana standing in the doorway. She appeared pale. He rose at the sight of her. Starting forward she said "Jack? Where is he?"

Denzil held the letter out to her, and she seized it reading rapidly. He watched her face as she read it, seeing her colour rise and then ebb again. Porth, a silent and interested audience of this by play was disappointed to receive an unmistakable sign from Denzil that his presence was to be dispensed with and withdrew reluctantly.

Viviana raised her eyes from the letter. "The matter must be urgent indeed to take him away in the middle of the night. Oh, I do hope that doesn't mean hostilities are to be renewed."

"Would you like some tea my dear?" asked Denzil

"No, coffee please —" She turned and walked to the window, staring out across the snow-covered lawn. He poured the coffee and watched her agitated pacing wondering, what had occurred last night. She had not returned from playing billiards with Jack and by the time he had emerged from the library at half past eleven, the house was quiet and there was no sign of either Viviana or Jack. Now this note from Jack.

"Your coffee my dear," he said offering the delicate cup. She turned back and took it, with a distracted smile, and he said "What is it? Has something upset you?"

She shook her head. "Why of course not. Except that I am disappointed Jack has gone. He is such fun, isn't he?"

"Yes, he is."

She turned back to the window with forced lightness. "Denzil I simply must go outside today. I am going mad penned in this house, please say you will let me."

"The ground is covered with snow, it is hardly advisable."

"I know but I must! Please!" she turned, put down the coffee and approached him, putting her hand on his arm. He covered it with his.

"It is futile to try to wrap you in cotton wool, isn't it?" he said with a smile.

"Yes, completely futile" she said with a strange laugh.

"Very well, but I am coming with you," he said firmly.

She looked out the window again but said nothing. He wondered what she was staring at.

AN HOUR later they were out on the snow-covered field, their horses picking a careful path across the white paddock. Her breath clouded in the cold air, as she took in great draughts of it, trying to clear the tightness in her throat. She had been feeling stifled and terrified since that explosive encounter with Jack. She had felt arousal in a man's arms before, Denzil aroused her, she wouldn't have consented to marry him if he didn't. Even the reprehensible Sir Anthony aroused her. There was something dangerous about that man that appealed to her. There had been moments during the season last year when she had toyed with the notion of marrying him. But Denzil was by far the better man, and she knew it. But then she had not met Jack.

Glancing at Denzil beside her, she compared the two brothers yet again in her mind. From the moment she had laid eyes on Jack she had felt the attraction. But last night had confirmed what she suspected since the incident with the riding crop. Not only was she attracted to him far more than she was to his brother, but he was equally and powerfully attracted to her. And he had left because of it. Because of her.

She kicked her horse into a gallop and took off across the field. She heard Denzil call to her in sudden alarm, but she didn't care. Yes, it was dangerous to gallop over snow, hidden rabbit holes or tree roots could bring down horse and rider in such conditions, but she couldn't stay still!

Her mare, Lady, her limp cured and fresh from too many days pent-up in the stable was as ready for a gallop as her mistress, and responded to her kick with alacrity. In moment's they were away across the field and setting at a fence looming rapidly. Lady gathered and leaped, clearing the fence easily. Leaning close over the mare's withers she set herself at the next fence, exhilarated by the speed. But as the fence came closer, some unevenness in the ground must have thrown the mare, because the leap went awry, and she was flung sideways and forward, tumbling with the momentum of the ride, and landed on her back on the snow.

She was winded but otherwise unhurt and lay looking up at the patchy sky trying to get her breath as Denzil flew over the fence, brought his horse to a rearing halt and flinging himself from the saddle ran to her side.

Kneeling in the snow he bent over her. "God Viviana, are you mad?"

It was such an echo of his brothers demand a week earlier that she was seized with the desire to laugh, but breathlessness prevented her. She gasped, trying to catch her breath.

"Are you hurt?" he said anxiously feeling her gently for broken bones.

She shook her head and managed to whisper, "Winded"

She got her breath at last and closed her eyes a moment, opening them as he said, "Serves you right!"

She did laugh then, it was so much like something Jack would say and not what she expected from Denzil. He added exasperated, "What am I going to do with you?"

She smiled. "Whip me and put me on bread and water for a week until I mind you as a good wife should."

He smoothed a lock of hair from her face tenderly. "I could never do that." His expression had sobered, and she fought the sudden urge to cry. How could she think of Jack when Denzil loved her so? She held out her arms. "Help me up, I'm getting wet."

He helped her up, retrieving her horse and checked the mare for a sprain or break; miraculously she appeared unhurt. Boosting her into the saddle he stood with his hand on her bridle, while she patted the mare soothingly. "Viviana, how can I stop you doing crazy things?"

"You can't," she said simply, staring down into his face, her eyes misting in spite of herself. "I don't deserve you Denzil," she whispered and pulling the reigns taught, she circled Lady, set her at the fence and rode hard for the house.

. . .

DENZIL, following behind her, was conscious of a resurgence of anger. By the time he reached the stables she had disappeared into the house. He followed her determined to have it out with her. This sort of behaviour couldn't go on. After the incident with Tempest, he had thought her penitent. But clearly, she was not. Entering via the side door, he went through to the main hall and saw her hurrying up the stairs to the upper floor. He called her name and taking the stairs two at a time caught her on the point of entering her room.

"Viviana!" he pulled her round to face him and was confronted by tears. Disarmed, his anger evaporated, and he said, "My dear what is it?"

She pulled away from him. "Nothing Denzil! Just leave me alone!" Whipping round, she opened her bedroom door and slammed it in his face.

Staring at the wood panelled door he debated for perhaps half a second opening it and demanding an explanation. But she wasn't his wife yet. And they were creating just the sort of ill-bred scene he abhorred. Instead, he went to his own room to change and then to his study.

He had enough estate business to keep him occupied and it was better than sitting around waiting for Viviana to recover her temper. And he had never been so close to losing his with her. For the second time since his engagement, he had doubts about the wisdom of this alliance. For the first tine he questioned his own feelings. Had he fallen victim to an infatuation? He had thought he loved her to distraction, but did she love him? She showed so little regard for his feelings or desires that he was beginning to doubt it.

He put down his pen and stared sightlessly at the pile of papers in front of him. Had lust and affection blinded him to her faults? They had to do better than this. He pushed his chair back and stood up going out into the hallway. Had she come down yet? It was unlike her to stay in her room for long. He checked the parlour and the morning room and library, but she wasn't in any of them. Neither Mary nor Lady Hartley had not come down yet and the house felt oddly silent and empty. He stood in the middle of the hall hesitating.

Finally, he went up the stairs and knocked gently on her door. There was no answer and he turned away. Perhaps she was sleeping? It was almost mid-day. Something nagged at him. He turned back and knocked again calling her name. Still no answer. The conviction that she wasn't there grew so pronounced that he opened the door before he could stop himself.

And he was right. The room was neatly made up and completely empty.

CHAPTER 10

*S*tanton was at the top of the stairs when the doorbell rang. He reached the bottom as the door opened to reveal Sir Anthony Harcourt standing on the step.

He smiled and stepped over the sill into the hall before Denzil could take evasive action. *Damn the man! Could the timing be worse?* He strode across the hall and held out his hand, ever the polite host.

"Harcourt. What brings you here?"

"Stanton." The two men shook hands and Porth took Harcourt's hat, gloves, muffler, and heavy overcoat. "You may recall I threatened to pay you a visit before I left London." Harcourts tone was smooth. "I have spent an interminable three weeks in the wilds of Northumberland, amongst my relatives. My grand sires temper being somewhat uncertain I am in need of sensible company. Will you take pity on me Stanton?"

Swallowing his annoyance Denzil tried to smile and waved his unwelcome guest towards the morning room with a signal to Porth. "Certainly, Sir Anthony, will you stay to lunch?"

"I would love to my dear fellow" said Harcourt with unwonted affability, passing through the door, Stanton held for him and into the parlour. Denzil gritted his teeth and smiled woodenly.

The fire in the room had been recently lit in anticipation of Lady Hartley and Mary's emergence from the bedroom and was doing its feeble best to dispel the overnight chill. a sudden flurry of snow hit the window pain and an errant draft made the flames in the hearth jump and dance. The clock on the mantle showed that it lacked a few minutes to mid-day. Harcourt cast a look around. "A pleasant room, will the ladies be joining us?"

Denzil opened his mouth to reply and was interrupted by the appearance of the footman with the drink's tray.

"Please take a seat Sir Anthony and have a drink to ward off the chill. If you will excuse me for a few minutes there is something I need to attend to." Without waiting for a reply Denzil ducked out of the room and crossed the hall to the stairs. Running up them two at a time he sought his sister's bedchamber, barely waiting for her acknowledgement before entering on the sound of his knock.

Mary was seated her dresser placing a cap carefully on her brown curls, seeing Denzil's face in the mirror she said quickly, "Tasker, you may go, stay, the green cambric wrap please!" Her dresser a very proper young woman with aspirations, placed this tenderly round her ladyships' shoulders and with a measured curtsy left the room, closing the door with tender mercy.

"Good heavens Denzil what has she done now!"

"That's the devil of it don't know!" said Denzil with the air of man about to tear his hair out. "We — quarrelled I suppose you would say, she went to her room and slammed the door in my face. I left her alone for, while to -"

"Stew?" interpolated Mary with a quizzical look.

"Recover" said the Earl with dignity, which made Mary smile. "I knocked on her door just now to see if she had repaired her temper and — she wasn't there!"

"Do you want me to look for her?" asked Mary with a soothing look.

"Well, I would except Harcourt is below in the morning room!"

"Good heavens Denzil didn't you have the sense to say we were not at home?"

"I was in the hall when Porth opened the door. I could hardly deny the man when he was staring at me over Porth's shoulder!"

"No, I suppose you couldn't! How vexatious. What can have brought him here at such a time?"

Denzil looked grim. "My assumption is he wishes to see Viviana!"

"Oh dear, yes you may be right. How absurd of him. He cannot expect to continue to prosecute his suit under your roof, it would be most improper!"

"Since when has that stopped him?" Denzil breathed out through his nose. "Anyway, I left him alone in the morning room. I had to asked him to stay to lunch. Will you go down and be polite to him for a few minutes while I try to find Viviana? I am concerned she may have taken her horse out again."

"Oh dear!" said Mary again, rising and clutching her reticule. "Yes, all right Denzil but don't leave me alone with that wretched man for long, I don't like him. Where's Jack anyway or has he run away too?"

"As a matter of fact, he has" said Denzil heading for the door.

"What!" said Mary dropping her reticule. "Not with Viviana?"

Denzil picked up the reticule and handed it to her. "No, no! He left last night, recalled to his regiment I believe."

"Oh no! Just when I thought we had him home for good!" said Mary following him down the stairs.

. . .

WHEN DENZIL SLIPPED BACK into the morning room, he found Mary making painful conversation with a politely bored Sir Anthony.

At sight of him, Mary interrupted her own rather convoluted story of a cousin's visit to India and said brightly, "Oh Denzil there you are! Will Viviana be joining us for lunch? Sir Anthony was just asking after her."

Denzil joined his sister on the couch and crossing one elegantly booted leg over the other said, "No I am afraid not. You will forgive her Sir Anthony, Miss Torrington has the headache."

Mary threw Denzil a speaking looking look out of the corner of her eyes. "Oh, I do hope nothing serious Denzil?"

"I hope not too," replied the Earl repressively.

Just then a log rolled out of fire onto the hearth. Seeing it Sir Anthony, who was closest to the fire in the winged chair facing the window, rose saying, "Allow me" and bent to attend to it with the fire tongs. He placed the log carefully back into place and hung the tongs back on their tree. Behind his back Mary arched her eyebrows in enquiry at Denzil, and he shrugged, his mouth compressing.

"What is this?" Asked Sir Anthony rising with a twist of paper in his hand. "Someone must have dropped it in the coal scuttle." The paper was slightly smudged with coal dust, but it was of good quality. He held it out to Denzil who took it with an odd feeling of unease. Harcourt's face was bland, yet Denzil had the impression he was amused about something.

"What is it Denzil?" asked Mary peering at the paper in his hand.

Denzil unscrewed the paper and read the words scrawled in haste across the page. His heart which had skipped a beat at the sight of the twist of paper thudded violently, and he felt his face flush. Turning away he shoved the paper into the pocket of his jacket. "It's nothing, a bill. I don't know how it got here. One of the servants must have picked it up by accident and dropped it."

He heard his own voice and thought that he was speaking nonsense. He felt as if the world had turned upside down.

"A bill Stanton?" said Harcourt. "How odd. But then servants do the most peculiar things don't they?"

"Yes -" said Denzil mechanically, staring out the window.

Harcourt turned to Lady Mary and Denzil heard him say, "My dear I fear Stanton is not well either. I think perhaps I should not stay to lunch after all. Please give my respects to Miss Torrington when you see her. No don't bestir yourself my dear, I will see myself out. Good day Stanton."

Denzil turned back to acknowledge him but made no attempt to stop him as he kissed lady Mary's hand and with a nod at Denzil left the room.

CHAPTER 11

*J*ohn and Hardy reached the Barracks in Westminster, by early morning, having ridden through the night. They were cold to the bone and both glad of the fire Hardy kindled in their quarters. Inured to much harsher conditions in the Peninsular, a few hours ride through a cold night was no real hardship to either of them, but Hardy had been enjoying both the comforts of the country house and a country housemaid and was not particularly happy to be parted from either one at such short notice. Listening with half an ear to his low grumbling monologue, Jack eventually said roughly, "Stow it grumble shanks! I had my reasons and there's an end of it!"

Hardy turning his attention from the fire, which was well alight now, to his masters' muddy boots, threw Jack a shrewd glance. "Soul of a lightskirt that one Captain, you're well out of it in my opinion."

"No one asked your opinion!" said Jack negotiating his chin carefully with the razor.

"Hmph!" said Hardy unpacking their bags and finding the blacking to clean the boots. "We headed back to the field Captain?"

"Not today Hardy. I will need to speak to the Commander. See if there is a commission for me."

"Hmph!"

Jack set down his razor and rinsed the soap off his chin, running his hand over it to check he hadn't missed any bristles. He was tired with that gritty aching feeling, like a sour taste in his soul. An hour later, dressed in his uniform, he presented himself at the office of the commander and asked if he would see him, only to be informed after a three-hour wait, that he was not at the Barracks today. The captain should come back on Thursday. The Commander might see him then. *Two days!* Chagrined but resigned, Jack headed back towards his quarters, but the thought of Hardy's surly presence made him veer off and head out to his club. He would seek a meal and perhaps a drink or two to drown his damnable bad temper.

Ensconced in a quiet corner with a plate of beef and a jug of porter he was three-quarters of the way through both when a voice pulled him from his sombre thoughts.

"Jack! Had enough rustication dear boy?"

He looked up from his plate into the mobile features of Ashley Morton. Rising he bowed punctiliously "Morton! What are you doing in London at this damnable season?"

Morton waved a thin white hand. "Had some business to finalise before heading into Bedfordshire to visit m'mother. Judging from the weather I may be here longer than I planned. I hear it is snowing heavily in the North."

Despite the fact that he didn't feel like company, Jack politely asked Morton to join him.

"Don't mind if I do. Club's dashed thin of company this time of year. Where's Den? Still entertaining his lady love?" said Morton pulling up a chair and waiving for a waiter.

Jack nodded, using the excuse of a mouthful of beef to avoid answering.

Morton ordered beer and shepherd's pie and settled in for a

comfortable evening with the words, "Don't mind admitting I'll be damned glad when the weddings over, and he's bedded that woman, Den's become a dead bore since he fell in love. Told him so myself."

Jack choked and Morton said solicitously, "Something caught in your throat?"

Jack shook his head and said hoarsely through a bout of coughing, "Swallowed the wrong way!" He took a draught of porter and signalled the waiter for another, which arrived with Morton's meal.

Tucking into the plate, Morton waved his fork. "Harcourt was the favourite right up to the last you know. Never expected the Torrington to show so much sense. Best thing she could have done, choosing Den over that blackguard."

Jack pushed his empty plate aside and continued drinking steadily. "Harcourt? Ranald Harcourt?"

"No, the grandson, Anthony. You may not have met him. Same cut as the old man."

Jack put down his tankard. "Harcourt was making up to Viv — Miss Torrington?"

"Oh yes. All the betting in the clubs was on Harcourt. We all thought she would take him. Well until Den threw his hat into the ring there wasn't any real competition. Harcourt will inherit when the old man pops off and the word is he won't last much longer." Morton took a long pull of his beer and eyed Jack solicitously.

"You all right Jack? You look a bit peaky."

Jack finished the porter and waived at a waiter. He needed something stronger. "Fine. I might have got a chill this afternoon. Tell me more about Harcourt."

Morton wiped his mouth and dropped his napkin on the plate. "Bad man. Well, you know his grandfather, don't you?"

The waiter returned with a bottle of whisky and two glasses

and poured for them. Jack took his and sipped the strong liquor. "Not formally, but I know his reputation."

"Well, the grandson's worse. Nasty piece of work. Killed more than one man in a duel its rumoured. Went through two fortunes by all accounts. Ruined Fenwick. That's what drove him to suicide, you know."

"Surely Miss Torrington's family wouldn't allow her to marry such a man?"

"Do you know Miss Torrington?"

"A little. I met her at Seven Oaks."

"Well by all accounts she is a wilful piece and her uncle and grandmother have no control over her. She received a lot of offers you know."

"Yes, I do know." Jack emptied his glass and refilled it offering Morton a top-up, which he declined with a shake of the head. John took another large mouthful and reflected he would have a devil of a head tomorrow. He watched the candlelight in the amber liquid. Had he been right to run away? Should he have stayed to brazen it out? Or told Den the truth? He shook his head. No, it was her decision. His feelings were irrelevant in the overall scheme of things. He would return to the continent and by the time he returned, if he did, this infatuation, this unbearable lust for a woman he had no right to, would have faded. Such intensity couldn't last.

Morton suggested a round of cards, and they played piquet to while away the afternoon, the whisky getting lower in the bottle. After dinner and a second bottle, Morton bade him good night and Jack thought muzzily he should retire himself. Making his way somewhat unsteadily out of the club, the cold night air made him reel a bit, and he held onto the wall to stop the pavement from dancing. Yes, he was drunk, thoroughly so. He hadn't been this cast away since Boney got stowed on Elba. Pushing himself away from the wall, he wandered down the street in quite the wrong direction from the barracks.

He emerged on Mayfair and stopped, blinking owlishly in the light of the street flambeaux, at the steps up to a tall narrow house. There was a light on in an upper storey indicating that there was someone in residence and still awake. He wondered why his feet had brought him here. Setting himself at the stairs, he climbed them and knocked on the door. After some time, the door was opened by his brother-in-law's Butler, Horace. Recognising Jack, he said "Captain Elliot, what –"

"Need to speak to Mary," said Jack carefully.

"Lady Mary isn't here Captain Elliot," said Horace patiently.

Jack blinked at him. "Of course, she isn't. She's at even Oaks. I knew that." He paused cogitating. "Leave her a note." He made as if to cross the threshold and was arrested by a voice from the stairs across the vestibule.

"Jack! What the devil-?"

Jack looked past the Butler to his brother-in-law, Wroxton, halfway down the stairs in a mulberry brocade dressing gown.

"Timothy!" said Jack "What are you doing here?"

Wroxton came down the last of the stairs and crossed the hall. "I live here, Jack." With a wave at Horace he murmured, "Make a bed up for the captain, will you? And send some porter up to the library." Horace bowed and disappeared and Wroxton shepherded his brother-in-law upstairs.

Having deposited Jack in an armchair in the library where he had been enjoying a late night read, his host took the high-backed chair on the other side of the fireplace. "What brings you here Jack?"

Jack rubbed his face. "I don't know. I just didn't fancy my rooms at the barracks."

An under footman arrived with the porter and poured. Jack eyed the beverage with a jaundiced look but accepted the proffered glass. Wroxton sipped his casually. "I wasn't expecting to see you in London. Everything all right at Seven Oaks?"

Jack drank the porter and it sobered him slightly. Enough to gather his wits and consider his words and his audience. Wroxton was no fool. He put down the empty glass. "Do you think Den will be happy?"

Wroxton compressed his thin lips a moment and said shortly, "No reason he shouldn't is there?"

Jack dropped his hands to his thighs with a slap and shrugged. "No, I suppose not." After a bit he added.

"You don't think Den and Miss Torrington will suit?" Jack looked up directly. "Do you?"

Wroxton flushed slightly and said gruffly, "Jack you're foxed!"

"I'm blue devilled!" said Jack frankly.

Wroxton looked alarmed. "Jack, what happened after I left?"

Jack stared at the flames in the fireplace morosely. "Nothing."

Wroxton shook his head. "Not nothing with you looking fit to cut your stick. What happened?"

Jack sat back in his chair and closed his eyes. "Have you ever been in love Timothy?"

"Hardly the sort of question to ask me, is it?" said Wroxton looking uncomfortable. "I love your sister of course-"

Jack opened one eye and looked at him. "Yes of course you do. It was the wrong question. Have you ever met a woman who turned you inside out?"

Wroxton drank the rest of his porter and refilled the glass, topping up Jacks. "No. And I'm glad of it. Women of Miss Torrington's stamp don't appeal to me."

"You're lucky" said Jack and drank some more of the porter.

Wroxton put down his glass with a slight thump. "For God's sake Jack what have you done? If you've poached on Den's turf and Mary gets wind of it -!"

"I haven't! I swear" Jack swallowed "I haven't, and I wouldn't. God-damn it Timothy, he's my brother!"

"Hmmp! Best stay away Jack. Women like that are trouble."

"Yes, I know," said Jack softly with his eyes closed. A few moments later his breathing told his host he was asleep.

. . .

"JACK, WAKE UP!" A hand shook him violently and Jack sat up with a start.

"What?" Jack blinked at his grim-faced brother-in-law. Alarmed he sat up straighter and rubbed his face. "What's amiss?"

Wroxton passed him a note. "This just came from Mary."

My Dear Timothy,

I very much fear that something has happened to both Viviana and Denzil. Viviana went missing this morning at around 10:00 am. Den refused to tell me at first, but then he received a most disturbing letter and nothing would hold him, but he must be off somewhere — I know not where, so don't ask me! He refused to show me the letter, provoking creature! He said that he was going to fetch her back. From his look I know he thought she was in some danger, but he refused to disclose the whole to me. He left at midday and it is past 6:00 pm now, and I am distracted with worry, for there has been no sign of either of them and no word from Denzil. And to make matters worse it has been snowing so hard I fear we will be snowbound by morning.

I beg you my dearest please come at once. I am very afraid that something has happened to them, Lady Hartley is prostrate with worry, I have had to call the doctor her palpitations were so bad. Please my dear come as soon as you may, or you will find the roads impassable.

Your loving Mary

PS: I almost forgot, Jack left in a hurry the night before. I do hope that had nothing to do with this. Perhaps if he is in London, you can call on him and ask if he knows anything to the purpose. I am worried sick with all three of them gone within hours of each other. I do hope that Jack reached London safely. Please send me word if you cannot come yourself.

PPS: I don't know if this has anything to do with it or not, but Harcourt called just before noon, it was he that found that wretched note!

CHAPTER 12

*S*tanton had been forced to slow the curricle to a walk for the last mile or so the visibility was so bad. The road was badly cut up in places too, making it rough going. The temperature had been steadily dropping and snow had begun to fall adding to the drifts on the side of the road and the covering on the fields. Alone in a white gloomy landscape with only his thoughts for company Denzil pushed on grimly, fuelled by a mix of anger and anxiety.

One of the horses stumbled and a wheel of the curricle fell into a pothole lurching and rocking as he negotiated his way over the uneven ground. It was rapidly becoming icy. This was getting dangerous and concern began to eat away his anger. The thought of her out here in these conditions -

The report of a gunshot made him and the horses start, and he looked around trying to penetrate the fog and swirling snow that obscured the road ahead and much of the landscape on either side of the road. Surely no poacher would be out in this weather? There came another shot. This time closer. The horses shied and came to a halt. He spoke to them quietly, but they remained spooked and refused to budge.

Getting down from the carriage he went to the leader's head and checked her fetlocks wondering if she had sustained an injury when the vehicle hit the pothole. Beauty nickered and blew hot air in his ear. He patted her comfortingly "I agree my lady, I would rather not be here either." He transferred his attention to her companion, conscious that his toes were growing numb in his boots as he stood in the growing snow on the road. The shoulders of his coat were already getting a generous sprinkling of white.

A third gunshot made the horse he was checking toss his head and neigh, his eye showing white. Beauty picked up her mate's fear and the lead pair shot forward, the second pair kicked and neighed too, the whole team suddenly galvanised, dragging the curricle forward and Stanton with it. "Woah!" he called. Grabbing the bridle, he struggled against the team pulling him forward, feeling the muscles in his arms pop with the effort of pulling them up by main strength from his disadvantaged position. Grunting and sweating he held on and bought them to a halt, stumbling over the uneven ground. Panting he hung onto the bridle getting his breath back. The horses stood still but they were thoroughly spooked, their withers quivering and their ears twitching.

The air was hushed and muffled, as if not only sight but also sound was blanketed by the snow and fog. He heard nothing, but a sixth sense, perhaps communicated by the horse's alarm, brought his head up, and he spun on his heel to be confronted by a masked man on horseback, wearing a heavy frieze coat and levelling a pistol at his head. He put his hands up and step backwards instinctively, away from the man and the horses.

"Good God sir what do you want?"

The man did not respond, just continued to keep the gun trained on him. He wore a hat pulled well down over his eyes, so that very little of his face was visible. Stanton took another step backwards and the world exploded with pain as a blow to the back of his head felled him where he stood.

CHAPTER 13

*V*iviana stared at the door she had slammed in
Denzil's face and dashed a hand across her cheeks
to wipe away the tears. Turning she went to fling herself on the
bed and stopped short. Something white caught her eye poking
out from under the carpet near the door. It must have been
shoved under the door, and she hadn't seen it earlier. It was a
single sheet folded in three. She picked it up and opened it, the
handwriting was firm and black. The words jumped and blurred
as she read through her tears.

*My Dearest Sister, (for that is what you will be when next we meet),
I wish you every happiness in your marriage, you have chosen the best
and most worthy of men. I was wrong to berate you for your high spirits
because it is that spirit in you that he loves so much, as must all who
know you. I have been recalled to my regiment and fear that I will miss
your wedding. Please forgive me. Jack*

She sat down on the bed abruptly, staring at the words, her
heart thumping wildly. The sharp sweetness of Jack's touch came
back in full force. She wanted — no, she *needed* him! She couldn't
marry Denzil. Not now that she *knew* –

She should go downstairs now and tell Denzil, tell him the

truth, he deserved that at least. But if she did, he would never let her go to Jack, and if she didn't go, he would leave, and she might never see him again...worse he would return to his regiment and he could be killed! At all costs she had to prevent that.

She bolted off the bed and went to her wardrobe, pulled out her cloak and found her purse attaching it to her belt. *What should she take? Anything? Nothing?* In the end she packed a small satchel with a change of clothes, toiletries and stuffed the note into the pocket of her riding dress.

With a pulse beating frantically in her throat she went to the door and cracked it open. The corridor was empty. She went to the stairs clutching the satchel in one hand and her skirts in the other, expecting at any moment to be stopped, but there was no one on the stairs, or miracle of miracles in the hall below. She ran lightly down the stairs and paused.

She must leave Denzil and Grandmama some explanation, so that they wouldn't worry, he would know she was safe and not pursue her. She flitted across the hall to the morning room, opened the door gently and finding the room empty, slipped inside. Going to the desk in the window embrasure she scribbled a hasty note, twisted it and propped it beside the mantle clock, which chose that moment to chime half past the hour. With her nerves jumping, she opened the door a crack, found the hall still empty and fled to the front door, lifted the heavy latch, and let herself out, carefully closing the door behind her. It was so heavy she was certain the noise would rouse anyone in earshot. But she was down the steps and across the snow-covered driveway and into the protection of the hedge with still no-one seeing her.

Concealing the satchel beneath her cloak she walked briskly round to the stable, demanded that the groom saddle her mare and was up on lady's back and out of the stable yard and across the field in short order. She would ride for the boundary fence, jump it, and head towards the road to London.

JOINING the London Road after two hours negotiating the back roads mired in a heavy snowfall, convinced at any moment that she would see Denzil behind her, she set Lady at a canter for some distance. Having made up some time she hoped, Viviana slowed Lady to a trot and then a walk. The sky was leaden with promise of more snow and the air heavy with fog but at least it wasn't snowing at this moment and the chill wind had abated. The road was empty in both directions, although there wasn't a great deal of visibility. And after looking over her shoulder every few yards for a while, she began to relax and settle into the gentle motion of the horse's gait, wrapped in the cocoon of the icy and eerily still atmosphere.

A further hour later she was daydreaming idly of what Jack would say when she appeared on his doorstep, when she heard the soft sound of horse's hooves on the snow behind her. In a panic she looked over her shoulder thinking it must be Denzil after all. To her surprise, two riders were bearing down on her. Each was muffled to the eyes in scarves, with great coats and wide brimmed hats, hiding their every feature from view. Neither of them appeared to be Denzil, but perhaps he had sent the grooms after her? Surely not he would be anxious to avoid a scandal. The horses they rode appeared to be of good quality, which gave her pause, and she turned back, kicking Lady into a trot and trying to reassure herself that these riders would over-take her with no more attention than they would a passing dray.

They did seem bent on overtaking her. The sound of their hooves grew louder and the pace increased. With her heart beating heavily and a tingling between her shoulder blades, she kicked Lady into a canter. She glanced back and her heart leaped into her mouth as the riders increased their pace too.

Lady lengthened her stride into a full gallop, and she leaned forward gripping tightly with her knees. The cold air burned her cheeks and throat, and she choked, as unreasoning panic ran up her spine. The riders were closing on her, the horses one dark and one grey, were big-boned brutes and their flying hooves ate up the distance between her and them. Lady was at full stretch now, but they were closing the gap.

There was a bend in the road up ahead, and she entertained wild thoughts of plunging off the road into the thickets on either side, but with the ground covered in snow it was too hazardous. She stuck to the road and rounded the bend, the two riders close on the mare's tail.

The first of the riders drew abreast of her and put out a gloved hand to seize her bridle. She lashed out at him, but her blow made no difference. His hold on the bridle tightened, and he slowly brought the mare to a halt, some five hundred yards past the bend. His companion rode up on the other side and crowded her. Her legs became wedged between Lady's flanks and the other horses. The first man on the dark horse, still had hold of Lady's bridle and the mare snorted and whinnied at the proximity of the other horses. He sniggered and speaking across her to his companion he said, "Nice prize this one!" the horses jostled one another and the men controlled their mounts with their knees. Viviana tried to pull Lady's bridle free of the man's grip and failed abysmally. Her mouth was dry, and she swallowed fear and cold air, her heart thumping.

"What do you want?" she asked, trying to steady her voice.

"What do I want, pretty lady? Well, that depends on what you've got, don't it?" said the voice from behind the muffler. He seemed to think this was funny and his companion agreed with him, both sat on their horses chuckling at their own wit and Viviana lost her temper.

"Well, I've got nothing for you!" and she swung her fist at his face. She took him by surprise and let go Lady's bridle in his effort to dodge the blow. Viviana kicked the mare forward and pushed free of the two men, but she didn't get far.

They caught and corralled her a second time and the spokesman said, "Now that's not polite pretty lady! Seems we'll have to teach you some manners!"

Just then she heard the sound of carriage wheels and horses from behind them, and she elbowed the dark rider in the ribs, hit out with her other hand at the others face and wheeling Lady, kicked her into forward motion and screamed at the top of her lungs. Round the bend in the road, came a private travelling coach, drawn by four good quality horses. Relief surged through her as she realised this equipage must belong to someone of means. The driver brought the team to a halt abreast of Viviana and her captors and the guard on the back of the coach levelled a blunderbuss at them. The pair took one look at this and wheeled their horses and road off, just as the door of the carriage opened and the figure of a tall man with red hair stepped down onto the road.

CHAPTER 14

The motion of the coach rocked its occupant gently, and her head nodded against the squabs. A weak shaft of sunlight broke momentarily through the clouds and slanting through the window, picked out the burnished copper colour of her hair. The face, framed by a neatly banded plait of that thick, deep-russet hair, was neither in its first youth nor strikingly beautiful. The nose was too thin and pointed, the chin too determined. But the lady's skin was fine and pale, and she possessed the unusual attribute, very rare in red heads, of dark brows and lashes. The lashes fluttered and opened, roused by a change in the rhythm of the coach's progress, and Miss Anne Harcourt, sat up, peering out the window through eyes of a deep vivid green. Her rather too generous mouth pursed, as she observed the white blanketed landscape, it had been snowing heavily in this part of the country for some time.

The brief glimpse of sun slipped behind the clouds, a heavy portentous grey; the sudden loss of light seemed to make the temperature plummet. Miss Harcourt had been travelling for several hours and her feet were thoroughly chilled. She moved them restlessly in her jean boots and burrowed her hands into her heavy serviceable cloak, pulling it more tightly round her.

It had been a dismal Christmas, and she was feeling unaccustomedly low at the prospect of returning to the only home she had. She couldn't quite believe that Anthony meant to throw her out now that he was getting married. But she could well believe that his bride would not welcome the idea of his sister remaining under the same roof. She grimaced. The idea appealed even less to her. She had always known this day would come she supposed. With no independent source of income, she faced the fact that she would need to seek a situation. The prospect had been exercising her mind since Anthony had put her on notice. She had been trying to decide which would be preferable: to seek an appointment as a governess or a companion. She was best fitted to be a chatelaine, but such a role would be ineligible for a single woman.

She wondered if perhaps she could pretend to be a widow? The more she thought about this the more attractive the notion became. If she were a widow, she would have far more freedom than if she remained known to be a single woman. She had no intention of seeking a role in a nobleman's household. As far as society was concerned, she would just disappear. It wasn't as if she had been an active member of the upper ten thousand for some time. Her brief London season was a distant memory. Having dodged the only proposal of marriage, she had been likely to get, she had retired to the country to manage her brother's house and remained there. The lifestyle suited her. Anthony only came home periodically, most of his time was spent in London or in the constant social round of visiting friends. That left her in peace for the majority of the time.

She shook herself, trying to dislodge the heaviness around her heart. She had always known it would come to this. She swallowed, blinking against the sudden sting of tears. There was no point in crying about it, she told herself crossly, that wouldn't change anything.

A sudden lurch of the coach and a shout, followed by a slewing sideways as the vehicle teetered perilously, made her grab the strap, her heart thumping wildly. *Had they lost a wheel or hit q snow drift?*

The coach continued erratically for a few moments and then stopped. Sitting forward she peered out the windows but could see nothing but the snow-covered countryside on either side of the road. A cry made her stomach drop, and she fumbled with the door handle. Pushing the door open cautiously she leaned out trying to see. There appeared to be another vehicle across the road ahead of them and her coachman and one of the post boys were descending from the seat. An accident? Most likely. She debated whether to stay in the carriage, but curiosity got the better of her. Someone might be hurt and need attention.

She pushed the door open and climbed down, the snow crunched under her boots as she walked along the side of the coach. One of the post boys was at the horses' heads, they stood with their heads down, their harness jingled as they moved restlessly in place, their withers shuddering in the cold.

The other vehicle was a curricle and the first post boy had gone to the heads of the other team.

Between her team and the others, she saw a snow-covered hump in the road. With a jolt she realised it was a body, her driver Bob Newell was bent over it. With a cry she ran towards him and looked down at the body of a man in his late twenties. He was well muffled in driving coat and scarf and his hat had come off. He was unconscious by the look of him: frozen most likely, judging from the amount of snow on him.

With a shock that made her faint, she recognised his face: *Stanton! God In heaven was he dead?* Her knees gave way as she knelt in the snow. His face was ashen and his eyes were closed, his lashes clumped with snowflakes and ice congealed around his nose. A patch of bloody snow behind his head indicated a head injury of some kind.

"Bob! Oh, God!! What happened?" she cried, reaching out with tentative hands.

"Don't touch him Miss Anne," said Bob. "He must have been set upon. We almost ran him down; if his carriage hadn't been across the road, I would have. Visibility's so poor I was almost on top of him before I even saw the horses.

"Is he dead?" she asked faintly, swallowing.

"I don't think so Miss. But we'd best get him out of this weather. Judging by the amount of snow on him, he's been out here a bit of a while.

"Yes of course! Put him in the coach, we must find the nearest Inn and get a doctor to him."

"Yes Miss, but is it proper to put him in with you?"

"Don't be so absurd Bob! This is Lord Stanton! The man is unconscious and like to die of we don't do something! Here –" she waved at the post-boy holding the coach horses "I'll take those, you help Bob with Lord Stanton. And don't stand there gawping! Hurry!" she stamped her foot in the snow and the two men bent to pick up his Lordship and deposit him in the carriage. Anne waved at the other post-boy. "Can you drive his lordships team?"

The lad who had been inspecting the beautiful team attached to the curricle gave it as his opinion that too right he could! "Well, be careful! No doubt they are valuable horses and his lord-ship will be very displeased if they are hurt!" said Anne balefully.

Anne gave the coach horses back to the first post boy and climbed into the carriage. Arranging his lordships head tenderly on her lap, she grasped the strap as Bob turned the coach and stared down at a face, she hadn't seen in over eight years. His Lordships lips were a trifle blue and his breathing was shallow. She pressed her fingers to his neck checking for a pulse, it was erratic and thready, and she felt tears of panic start to her eyes.

His skin was cold to the touch, and she smoothed the hair back from his forehead with a shaking hand. "Oh, please God, don't let him die!"

The coach went over a pothole, lurched, and she grabbed him to stop him sliding off the seat onto the floor. He groaned and opened his eyes, blinking at her muzzily.

"Oh, thank God!" she swallowed a sob. "You've been set upon!"

"Have I?" he said faintly. "Hurts — like the devil!"

"Hush lie still!" she grabbed him again as the coach lurched making him gasp with pain. "Oh, I'm sorry!" she said distressed. Her gown was covered with blood from the wound on the back of his skull. "I must bind the wound and stop the bleeding. I do hope it's not far to the Inn." But she was talking to herself because he had lost consciousness again.

The next ten minutes were the longest of Anne's life as she clung to her burden, trying to cushion him from the potholes in the rutted surface of the road, and prayed with every ounce of her soul that he not die in her arms.

They arrived finally at the small wayside Inn, where Bob and the post-boy carried his Lordship up to a bedchamber in the teeth of the landlady's protests. Anne, who was fast losing patience with Mrs Kennedy, snapped, "You will be well paid for your trouble Ma'am. This is the Earl of Stanton! Now stop your nonsense and tell me at once where the nearest physician is to be found?"

Mrs Kennedy her double chins wobbling like a gobble cock stopped in mid-flight and stared at Anne. "That it'd be Dr Haddon."

"How far away is he?" demanded Anne.

"Less than a half hour" chimed in her son Jed, who was enjoying the sight of his mama speechless.

"Good, then please fetch him at once!" said Anne preparing to ascend the stairs in the wake of his lordships body.

Mrs Kennedy was not so easily brushed off however and gathering herself, she put an arm across the banister. "And whom might you be Miss?"

"Lady Mary of course, his sister, now let me past!" said Anne furiously and ducking under Mrs Kennedy's plump arm she ran up the stairs to the best bedroom where Bob and the post-boy were about to place his Lordship carefully on the bed.

"Wait!" said Anne ducking round them to pull back the coverlets, so they could put him on the sheets. "Bob, we need to get his driving coat and jacket off! And his boots!" she waved the post-boy to remove the boots while she and Bob removed his Lordships coat and jacket. The latter was a struggle since it was a tight fit and every movement jostled his lordships head and made her fear for his reason, but at last they were able to lay him down in his shirt and breeches. Just as a robust girl with her mother's round features came in bearing a bowl of water and several towels. "Oh, thank you!" said Anne with real gratitude taking one of the towels and placing it gently under Stanton's head.

Miss Kennedy inspected the Earl. "Bleeding like a stuck pig ent he? Head wounds always bleed summat fierce. Well, we don't get such as yourself much here. Don't mind mum, she was a bit overcome, and she likes to order things just so. Dub up the possibles and she'll come round."

Anne stared at her fascinated and said faintly "Thank you, I think. Will you hold him on his side while I bathe the wound on his head? The doctor will dress it properly, but I must try to stop this bleeding!"

Having created a rough bandage with his lordships neck cloth, Anne sat down to wait for the doctor. His Lordship didn't regain consciousness during this vigil, and by the time Haddon came up the stairs, her nerves were in shreds. Haddon was a small spare man with thinning grey hair. She pounced on him as he came in the door explaining as best, she could what she had done for his Lordships comfort.

"He has bled a great deal and I fear there may damage to his skull! Please don't let him die!" she ended on a sob, covering her hand with her mouth.

Haddon looked at his patient. "I will do my best for your husband ma'am, but ultimately that is God's will." She lifted her hand to correct his misapprehension, but he didn't see her, and she dropped it reflecting that it might be best not to say anything. The circumstances of her arrival with the Earl, both of them without personal servants did look peculiar. He bent to look at the tourniquet and grunted. "Head wounds do tend to bleed a lot Ma'am, but they can look worse than they are. The real danger is in concussion. Now tell me what happened, has he regained consciousness?"

"Yes. Briefly in the carriage."

"Was he himself when he did so?"

"Yes, he seemed to be quite sensible."

The Doctor nodded. "Hmm"

"Is that good?" she asked tentatively.

"On the whole yes. But there can be complications later if there has been swelling of the brain. Only time will tell that." He checked Stanton's pulse and then pushed up each eyelid and checked the pupils in each eye. He checked his body for other injuries and then set about tending and rebandaging the wound. When he had finished, he said, "Make him as comfortable as possible, change the dressing daily until the wound heals and keep him still, particularly his head, for at least twenty-four hours. Give him this, it will help him sleep, that is the best remedy. He should wake of his own accord in a few hours, if he doesn't -" he hesitated "If he hasn't woken or is not himself by tomorrow morning, call me." He pursed his lips and touched his lordships skin. "I think you might find that he has taken a serious chill. How long was he in the snow for?"

"I- I don't know, some time I think."

"Hmm" he said again "Check his extremities for chilblains or worse. If he should develop a fever give him this." He reached into his bag and gave her another mixture to accompany the laudanum. She took the medicines and set them on the bedside table. "Keep him warm, plenty of fluids, ride it out." He summarised.

She nodded. "Th-thank you."

"Don't thank me 'till he pulls through ma'am. A chill has carried off more than one of my patients before now, and a cracked head can be tricky. Wait and see!"

She nodded and tried to stop her lower lip trembling as she followed him downstairs. She was being such a ninny. Pulling herself together with an effort she asked him for his fee and having found his Lordships purse during the past hour of waiting, was able to pay him. She sent Bob upstairs to undress his Lordship and requested a hot brick to be sent up for his feet. Then she went out to the stables to check on the horses. Having satisfied herself that they had been properly tended to and were showing no signs of hurt, she went back up upstairs to change her bloodied gown. Having done that, she went to see her patient. Bob was standing by the bed watching him. She came in quietly and said softly, "I will stay with him Bob. Can you ask Mrs Kennedy to send up a tray for me later?"

"I will that Miss Anne." Rumbled Bob softly. "You call me if you need anything."

She nodded "Make sure you get fed too Bob and keep an eye on those post-boys. I don't know how long we will be here. It might be best if you paid them off?"

"No point Miss, they can't go anywhere. The doctor said the London Road is closed North of St Albans, the snows that heavy. We won't be going anywhere for a while I'm thinking."

"Oh." She nodded and went to the bed. She heard Bob go out quietly and took a seat beside the bed. The covers were drawn up to his chin and he was lying on his back like an Egyptian mummy, the bandage round his head and buried under a generous layer of blankets. She felt his forehead. It was warm, but not burning yet. She lifted the covers, adjusting them. His chest was bare, showing a neat expanse of slightly curling brown chest hair. Lifting the coverlet, a little more, she realised with a flush that the rest of him was naked also. She dropped the coverlet carefully back into place, scandalised at her own boldness. What if he woke and caught her looking at him? How would she explain that?

He seemed to be well and truly unconscious though, so she sat down and prepared to watch and wait. She spent the time inventing conversations with him, should he wake and demand an account of her presence in his bedchamber.

Would he even remember her? They had stood up for several dances at Almack's during her London season. They had been in the same room at several parties, she had even attended a ball at Elliot house on the occasion of Lady Mary's debut, but while she had treasured every moment they breathed the same air, she doubted that her presence had had the slightest impact on him.

As she sat and watched him in his comatose state, her school-girl dreams so long suppressed, came flooding back, bringing a wistful longing in their wake. She tried to shake them off, it was all nonsense. She was a grown woman now, quite on the shelf in fact. He, on the other hand, a few years older, was in his prime, an eligible bachelor. It seemed distinctly unfair, but that was the way of things and not much point in lamenting it.

Her mind came back around to its obsession. What would he say when he woke up and found her here? Would he feel compelled to make her an offer out of chivalry? Her heart contracted with the thought. Could she bear that? She shook her head, gripping her hands in her lap. No, she couldn't. This wouldn't do. She needed something to occupy her mind. She looked around wondering if this room boasted a book, a bible even....

She went to get up and look, but a movement caught her eye

and she realised that he had stirred and the coverlet had come away from his neck. She reached to tuck it back in and felt the heat coming off him. She felt his skin, it was hot and dry. As she held her hand to him, she felt his body tremble. The fever the doctor had warned of was taking hold.

She had little leisure for daydreaming after that. Her concentration being on keeping him covered and wiping his face with a dampened cloth. His restlessness was punctuated by incoherent speech at times and at one point his eyes opened, and he grasped her hand tightly saying "Don't run from me again! We must do better than this!" Caught in the mesmerising grip of his fevered glare she stared into his face stupidly.

"Denzil I would never run from you!"

This seemed to quiet him for a while, because he closed his eyes and slept a little. But the fever dreams recurred, and she found herself sitting on the side of the bed, her hand gripped in his. It was the only way to keep him still. Each time she tried to ease out of his grip he would start awake and seize her. Gail Kennedy brought her supper up on a tray, but she didn't get the leisure to eat it.

In his more lucid moments, she got him to drink, lifting his head gently and holding the cup for him. It was like caring for a child, she reflected. Not something she was accustomed to. Towards dawn, he fell into a comatose state again and exhausted herself, she fell asleep on the coverlet beside him.

SHE WOKE WITH A START, as a shaft of sunlight fell on her face from between the curtains. She sat up on one elbow, looking at the man beside her. His body was warm and hers was cold and stiff. The temptation to crawl under the covers with him was strong. She lay a moment, allowing herself the luxury of a little fantasy, her body flushing slowly with warmth at the thought of sharing his bed. She was shocked at herself and exhilarated at the same time. Her body coiled with heat and tension. She let out a silent breath, trying to relieve the feeling.

He was sleeping heavily, and she sat up gingerly trying not to disturb him. She had just eased her feet to the ground when his eyes opened, and he blinked at her. He murmured, "I dreamed of an angel with green eyes in the snow and there you are." His eyes closed again, and she got up letting her breath go.

She went to find Bob to come and sit with the patient, while she sought her own room and some equilibrium. If anyone were to know that she had spent the night in his Lordships room, her reputation would be entirely ruined. She stared at herself in the mirror and grinned with idiotic delight. Who was she fooling? She was ruined already. It was absurd really, Stanton was in no state to take advantage of her, no matter how much she might wish he would. She blushed and turning away from the mirror began to strip, giving herself a Spartan cold flannel wash. Shivering she redressed and went downstairs to find some breakfast. After a solid meal she went back upstairs to check on the patient. Finding him still sleeping, she told Bob she was going to sleep herself and to wake her at need. Bob looked at her thoughtfully. "Yes Miss Anne."

She opened her eyes at him. "What?"

He shook his head. "Nothing Miss Anne." He looked back at Stanton. "If he weren't dead to the world, I'd think otherwise, but it's obvious he can't do you no mischief even if he wanted to. But if the Master catches wind o' it there'll be hell to pay."

"You won't tell him Bob?"

"Course not Miss Anne." He frowned. "All a same, you be careful Miss, I'd not like to see you hurt."

She smiled. "Thank you, Bob, I'll be careful."

Bob looked rueful and shook his head. "No, you won't. I've seen the way you look at him."

CHAPTER 15

*V*iviana, her heart beating heavily stared at Sir Anthony with mixed feelings. How could she explain her presence all alone on the road? He had been the most persistent of her admirers. She had not been immune to his charm and had seriously contemplated accepting his suit. There was something in his air of ruthlessness that appealed to her restless spirit. He couldn't compare to Jack of course. But back then she hadn't met Jack. She hadn't seen Anthony since her engagement to Denzil had been announced, did he know? Or had he left London before the announcement had appeared in the Gazette?

"Madam, may I be of assistance -" he stopped appearing to recognise her. "Miss Torrington! What -"

She decided to brazen it out. "Your arrival is most timely! I am on my way to London, and those ruffians seemed bent on stopping me."

"On your way to London, on horseback, all alone in this weather?"

She licked her lips nervously, the tone in his voice set a tremor beating in her throat. "Yes, I kn-know it sounds absurd, but circumstances m-made it imperative that I do so." She swallowed and lifted her chin, gazing up at him with defiance. God knew what he was thinking, his eyes appeared inscrutable, only the twitch at the corners of his mouth gave her the impression he was enjoying a private joke at her expense.

"My dear, there is no need to dissemble, I know the reason for your flight."

"Y-you do?" her breath caught in her throat and her heart thundered.

"Of course." He stopped and watched her with open amusement now, his air very much that of an uncle entertained by a youthful niece. He lowered his voice. "I read your note you see."

"My — my note?" she felt the blood drop to her feet and thought for a moment she would fall off her horse and then as rapidly she felt herself flushing at the glint in his eye. She gripped the bridle and said faintly. "Sir Anthony I don't understand!"

He continued to smile. "I must applaud your decision my dear. Stanton is a very dull dog. Still, no harm done, you have discovered your mistake before it was too late. I must say however that this flight is somewhat ill-judged. Should it become known you would be ruined my dear."

She remembered to breath suddenly. "If I can reach London tonight no one need know."

"Except me of course!" he said with a smile that made her shudder suddenly. 'Fortunate is it not, that I happened to come upon you just now? I will take you to London my dear, you really can't ride on alone, it is by far too dangerous as you have just experienced. But for my timely intervention no doubt your body would have been found in a snowdrift on the morrow!"

This catalogue of disasters made her suppress a shiver.

She refused to admit he was right. Forcing a smile, she said with an attempt at lightness. "You sound like Denzil! He was always convinced I would come to harm. I am perfectly capable of taking care of myself you know. It was unfortunate that those men came upon me. But your arrival drove them off easily enough"

"My dear I assure you, I am nothing like Denzil. I have far more respect for your — ah — independent spirit. All the same I must insist you let me take you to London. My carriage is warm and dry and will get you there in comfort and safety."

She opened her mouth to say no, and he added gently, "Please? I really can't in all conscience leave you here. No gentleman would leave a lady stranded in this weather."

His blue eyes held her pinned, and she found herself nodding and allowing him to hold Lady's bridle while she dismounted. He helped her up into the carriage steps saying,

"One of my men can ride your horse"

She turned on the step. "Thank you."

A few minutes later he joined her in the carriage, the steps were let up and the equipage lurched into motion.

SHE SETTLED into her corner of the carriage and wondered what he was thinking. If he had read her note — her head reeled with speculation — how had he come to read her note? What had happened after she left Seven Oaks? She glanced at him as he lounged at ease in the other corner, about a foot of space between them on the seat. Her heart was beating fast and an unaccountable nervousness had her in its grip.

She cleared her throat. "How did you come to read my note?"

"I was passing Seven Oaks my dear and called into see you. I found your note in the coal scuttle, it must have fallen off the mantle-piece."

"Oh, how-how odd." She gripped her hands in her lap.

"Did Denzil read it?"

"He did."

"And how did he react?"

"Denzil is by far too much the gentleman to show his emotions my dear.

"Yes of course." Her heart thumped a little lick of disappointment unfurled in her breast. She should be relieved if Denzil wasn't concerned for her after all, but a touch of pique made her lips tighten.

He smiled lazily at her. "In the normal course of events it should take about four hours to reach London from here, but with this weather..." he shrugged eloquently. "We shall have to keep ourselves entertained. What do you suggest?"

She, let out a breath of relief, glad to be distracted from her thoughts. She nodded at a book lying open face down on the opposite seat "You were reading, what is it?"

"Pamela or Virtue Rewarded, by Richardson, have you read it?" he reached for the volume and keeping a finger in his place, held up the spine for her to read, it was volume one.

"Yes. I read it last year, Grandmama told me it was not a proper book for me to read, so of course I read it."

He smiled "Of course. What did you think of it?"

"Pamela dithered too much, I was willing her to be more decisive!"

He grinned at this, showing even white teeth. "I feel sorry for Mr B. Does she ever let him have his way with her?"

"Oh, I won't give away the ending!" replied Viviana "Where are you up to?"

"He has just climbed into bed with her dressed as the maid!"

She choked on a giggle. "I really did think that was rather absurd!"

"Did you? How would you recommend a man seduce an unwilling woman then?" he asked, putting the book down and leaning forward slightly.

"If she is unwilling, he shouldn't be trying to seduce her at all!" responded Viviana a frisson of panic skittering down her spine.

"But was Pamela unwilling? Really?" he asked picking up her hand.

She tried to pull it away immediately, but he hung onto it a moment longer before relinquishing it. "I can't tell you that without giving away the ending" she replied.

"Tell me my dear, why did you refuse my offer?"

"Sir Anthony it is hardly fair to attempt to prosecute your suit in these circumstances!"

"I can hardly think of better my dear. You can't fob me off or send me to fetch you glasses of wine!"

She glanced at him and something in his eyes made her question why she had found him so attractive in the first place. He moved a little closer and took her hand again. "Viviana, you are the most bewitching woman I have ever met, and I love you to distraction. Marry me, please. Say you will."

She stared into his eyes a rising feeling of panic threatening to engulf her. "Anthony I can't!"

"Why not?" His eyes held hers, compelling her to answer. Her fingers twisted in his grip and he touched her face lightly with his other hand, tracing a finger along her jaw.

Her pulse leapt under his touch, and she said faintly, "You're frightening me!"

His mouth twitched and his eyes ran over her face. "It's not me you're afraid of, my sweet."

She took a breath and said firmly, "Anthony it is quite reprehensible of you to take advantage of me like this!"

"Yes, it's extremely unfair of me, isn't it? But then I never was one to play by the rules! I didn't think you were either." He leaned closer, and she withdrew pressing back into the squabs. His mouth hovered over hers and then pulled back.

"Well, are you?" he asked softly.

She said breathlessly, "Anthony please stop this!"

His eyes lingered on her lips for an interminable moment, and then he sat back with an air of humouring a child. "Very well my

Pamela." He smiled. "I would bet that she has him in the end. His persistence will have worn her down."

She relaxed a little in her seat now that he had withdrawn. "You will have to read to the end to find out. I won't spoil it for you."

"Do you play piquet Miss Torrington?" he said producing a pack of cards from his pocket.

With a sigh of relief, she said, "Yes I do."

"Do you play well enough to give me a challenge?" he asked shuffling and dealing out the cards on the seat between them.

She picked up her hand and sorted it rapidly. "I'd like to think I do."

"What would you care to wager on the game?"

"I have nothing of value on me Anthony, only some coins in my purse."

"I will play you for something of far greater value than gold."

Her heart turned over at the tone in his voice, and she knew what he was going to say. "I will not play you for a kiss Anthony, it would be most improper!"

"I wasn't going to suggest that my dear."

"You weren't?" she felt the oddest sense of being off balance.

"No. I will play you for a secret."

"W-what secret?" she asked staring at him suspiciously over her fan of cards.

"The secret to your heart my darling," he said playing his first card.

She managed a laugh. "Anthony that is absurd!"

"Is it? But my dearest it is the only thing I want," he said plaintively.

She shook her head which made one of the pins come undone and spill a thick black curl of hair forward over her shoulder. She played a card and pushed the curl back behind her ear.

They played in silence and the cards ran fairly evenly. She won the hand and dealt again. The light was gradually fading outside, but there was still enough to see by. He won the second hand. "Well, we are even. The best of three my dear? We will run out of light after that I fear," he said.

She nodded and he dealt the cards again. The cards appeared to be in her favour at the start, but she realised that she had made a fatal error on the third discard when he trumped her Queen. It was all downhill after that, and she lost the round resoundingly.

He gathered up the cards in the growing murk and put them back in his pocket. "Well, my dear will you pay your wager?"

"I never agreed to the stake!" she replied sharply.

He had moved close enough to take her hand again, but in the increasing gloom she could only make out his features in outline and the gleam of his eyes. She supposed her own features were equally shadowed to him. With the loss of visual cues her sense of smell sharpened, and she detected the scent of him.

"Shall I begin?" he asked quietly out of the dark. Her hand quivered in his and he said, "Shall I tell you the secret of my heart?" he turned to face her, the outline of his head was limned in silver from the external lights on the carriage. His knee nudged her thigh, and he played with her hand in his.

The movement of the carriage threw light from the lamps occasionally across his face. "I never thought that I would say this to any woman. But love makes fools of all of us, does it not?" His tone was low. "Like Queen Mab you have stolen my heart and my reason. Grant me my dearest wish, tell me that you will have me as master of your heart; for you are queen and mistress of mine."

She swallowed panic licking her skin. She should never have consented to get in his carriage. How could she have been such a fool as to trust him?

He leaned closer, and she scrunched back into the corner of the carriage. "Let me show you my beauty…."

Turning her hand over he pressed his lips into her palm, they were warm and dry and left an impression tingling on her skin. "We can deal together well my dear," he said softly, kissing the inside of her wrist. It was an intimate gesture that sent a bolt of pure terror through her. She tried to pull her hand away, but he held onto it and putting his other arm around her, pulled her against him and kissed her. She froze, tried to push him away. She had dreamed of Jack kissing her like this. Had lain awake aching for him to do so. *Jack!* She tried to evade his lips, twisting her face away, but he gripped her jaw forcing it back. A shudder passed through her.

The memory of Jack holding her against him, the heat and hardness of him pressed against her rump and the sweet tenderness of his lips against her neck, his hand warm and firm against her belly, had made her body weep with longing.

With an effort she pulled away from Harcourt's mouth, her own breathing quickened with fright. "No Anthony!"

"But yes! My Pamela!" he said capturing her mouth again and pressing her back into the squabs. She twisted her face away, and he whispered in her ear, "You came with me beautiful lady. I knew you would. We are alike you and I, I know you heart, better than you do."

She gasped and hissed in his ear, "No you don't! Let me go!" with which she bit his earlobe hard enough to make him pull away and swear.

"Bitch! Do you like it rough? Is that it?" His handsome face developed a shadow that sent a shiver down her spine and his hands on her squeezed like iron bands. He was a big man, and she realised with sudden shock that he was very strong. Her heart thumped against her ribs, and for the first time, real fear slithered over her skin.

She gasped, "No! I said No!" She felt the heat of tears sting her eyes. This man was ruthless and dangerous. She knew that. It had always been part of his attraction for her, but suddenly she realised just how vulnerable she was alone with him in this carriage.

In the next moment the look that had frightened her

vanished, and he lessened his grip on her arms, and he said soothingly, "I'm sorry! Blame the red hair, I have a temper, it gets the better of me sometimes. My sister says it gets into my blood and makes me impossible."

"You have a sister?" she said faintly.

"Yes Anne. She keeps house for me." He had drawn back but still kept his hand on hers, where it lay in her lap. "But don't worry, when we are married, she will live elsewhere. She is already making plans."

Something out the window caught her attention and she sat forward, looking through the misted-up glass into the dark. "That sign post — has the coachman missed his way? We are going in quite the wrong direction for London!" she turned to face him "Where are you taking me?"

"My house of course. We will be there quite soon."

"Have you run mad? This is abduction! You promised to take me to London!"

"Technically I didn't promise, I offered."

"That's a quibble, you led me to believe you would take me to London."

"Yes, I know, I'm sorry, but I assure you my house is most comfortable, and we can be married as soon as we arrive."

"What? No!"

"Well, yes. I have a special license in my pocket, and we will be married as soon as I can get you in front of a clergyman."

She shook her head as if to shake off a nightmare. "Anthony you can't, I can't, this is madness! You don't want a reluctant wife, I'll drive you crazy!"

"You already drive me crazy sweetheart. I want you so much I can't sleep at night."

"And my fortune has nothing to do with it of course!" she snapped.

"No, that is just a bonus. You can rest assured I want you for your sweet termagant self!" he said frankly.

"Why should I believe anything you say, you have already proved that you lied to me!"

"Well, that was necessary to get you into the carriage. But I meant what I said, I wouldn't and couldn't leave you to find your own way to London. Believe me, your fate with me is much more pleasant than what could have befallen you. By the way, why the mad scramble to go to London? What is in London that you want so desperately?"

"I-I was returning to my uncles house."

"Now who is lying? Your Uncle is at his country house, and you know that as well as I do. Let me tell you what you were going to London for shall I? Remember I read your note my dear. You didn't say so, but I am guessing that you are following Stanton's brother, the dashing Captain Jack Elliot. Am I right? I've never met him, but the housemaid said he was very handsome. He's the reason you broke it off with Stanton, isn't he?" He leaned forward, his tone taking on an ugly note that made her shake with temper and fear.

Temper won and she said, "Yes, you're right! And that's why I can't marry you!"

His voice dropped and developed an edge. "So, the Captain has been poaching on his brothers preserves, has he?"

She didn't answer, pressing back into the squabs of the coach just as the wheels lurched over a pothole and threw her against him. He grasped her upper arms. "Are you a virgin still or have your whorish instincts got the better of you?"

She wrenched an arm free and slapped his cheek hard. "How dare you!" Her heart hammered against her ribs, two parts fury to one part fear. *What would he do? Slap her back?*

He touched his raw cheek with one hand and surprised her by laughing. Laughter transformed his face, and she felt as if she were losing her footing. This man was not one shade of black, but as variegated as a peacock. Dangerous, ruthless, selfish, and even cruel probably, but he would protect what was his, and he was capable of a charm that had disarmed her initially, before she met Jack.

"You are a rare jewel, Viviana." He said with sincerity.

"Why, because I hit you?"

"Because I made you angry enough to hit me. For all your wiles you have an honest streak. I like that. I am also glad to know the captain hasn't stolen your maidenhead. I would have to kill him if he had, and you might find that a trifle difficult to forgive."

She shivered and he leaned forward, picking up a rug lying on the opposite seat and tucked it round her legs, all solicitude for her comfort. His hands lingered on her thighs, squeezing slightly through the layers of blanket, petticoated gown and cloak. He kissed the corner of her mouth and murmured, "Teaching you the delights of love will be the greatest pleasure of my existence, I think."

She shuddered again and tried to dodge his kiss. His hands on her thighs he pinned her to the squabs and pressed his mouth to hers. She twisted again under him, putting up her hands to push him away. *Jack!* She cried silently how could she free herself from this predicament? She had to find some way to turn the tables on this man, use his weakness against him.

He lifted his head to gaze into her eyes, his own still lit with that inner fire that threatened to eat her alive. His skin was flushed and his breathing quick. "Viviana these next hours will be the longest of my life until I can make you mine. No woman has ever stirred me as you do. Are you a succubus from hell come to taunt me?" He loomed over her, filling her whole view, he smelt of horse and leather and fragrant tobacco, mixed with a hint of male musk. She thanked heaven that there was no scent of alcohol on his breath. If he had been drunk there would have been no stopping him at this point.

She forced a laugh, struggling to find her old flirtatious self. "A succubus Anthony? I am hardly flattered by the comparison."

129

"An angel from heaven then? Come to teach me respectabil-ity? I swear I will turn respectable for you," he teased, his face showing her an expression made up of lust and something else — affection? Such a thought sat oddly with her idea of him. But she had already concluded that he was more complex, than at first, she'd thought.

"Much more flattering, but I fear not a promise you could keep," she responded, reaching for a playful note.

"Could I not? Am I challenged then?" He seemed willing to pick up the gambit of the game. Safer territory than kisses that spelled her ruin.

"You are offering me a fantasy irresistible to all women," she said. "A picture of the reformed rake giving up his reprobate life-style for the love of a good woman!"

"Irresistible to all women, except you, it would seem!"

"But as you pointed out I am not a good woman!" she replied.

"You are more than good enough for me." He said kissing her fingers and then licking her forefinger in a way that made her body shudder. She stifled a gasp of revulsion and tried to pull her hand away. "Anthony don't!"

"Call me Tony," he said kissing her jaw.

"I swear you won't regret your choice my dear," he said softly in her ear. She murmured something unintelligible. *Jack!* Behind her closed lids she saw his face, as she had last seen it torn apart by desire and horror at what they were doing to his brother. Despair assailed her. It really didn't matter if he loved her or not. He would get over it. She wasn't worthy of either of the Elliot brothers. She had to think, how could she escape Harcourt clutches. She had no desire to be ravished in a coach in the middle of a snowstorm.

Gently she pulled back and said steadily, "Anthony stop! Please! For decencies' sake we should wait until we are married!"

His eyes devoured her face with a molten lust that terrified her.

"Did you think I would deflower you here in the coach? I have more finesse than that my dear." He sat back, easing his legs out, but keeping hold of her hand.

How this night would end she didn't know, but she would play the game to the hilt and if she could, she would best Sir Anthony at his own gambit. Jack was beyond her reach now unless some miracle occurred. Could she rescue herself from this predicament? She had to try.

CHAPTER 16

*A*nne returned to Denzil's room, much refreshed from her sleep and relieved Bob of his sentry duty. In hushed tones Bob volunteered the information that his Lordship slept through, his fever seemed to have abated. Concerned, Anne sent him away to his lunch and wondered what she should do. Was it reasonable that he slept this long?

She bent over him and felt his forehead. Bob was right he didn't feel hot. She smoothed the hair from his forehead and saw his eyelids flutter. He opened his eyes and stared at her. She checked his pupils remembering the doctors' comments that enlarged pupils were a sign of — what had he called it? Concussion. They seemed a reasonable size and both were the same size which was also important the doctor had said. He blinked at her as if trying to bring her into focus, and she said, "How do you feel?"

"My head hurts." He pushed the coverlets away to free his hand and touched his head "Someone cracked me a beauty, didn't they?"

She bit her lip, on a wry smile, trying to suppress the tears of relief that welled in her eyes. He seemed sensible at any rate. "Yes, they did."

He lowered his hand and held it out. "I am afraid you have the advantage of me Madam, you look familiar, but I'm at a loss for your name, should I know it?"

"Anne Harcourt. You know my brother, Anthony."

The mention of her brother's name had a galvanising effect. "Harcourt! Good God!" He moved his head in an attempt to sit up and subsided with his eyes closed as his face went white.

Frightened she said, "Please, the doctor said you need to keep your head still! He said you may have something called concussion!"

He swallowed and breathed carefully for a few moments and then finally opened his eyes. "Yes, he may be right. I do feel rather nauseous. I understand that is one of the symptoms."

She nodded "Yes, he did say that. How do you know?"

"My younger brother John fell out of tree and concussed himself. I remember the ordeal quite well. He recovered," he smiled reassuringly at her. "I'm sure I will as well. Especially with such a fine nurse. Please tell me Miss Harcourt, where are we and how did we come to be here?"

She explained how she had come upon him in the snow and brought him here. She ended by saying with a blush, "I have led the Inn-Keeper and her family to believe that I am Lady Mary, it seemed best, given that we arrived together with no personal servants and -"

"Looking after the proprieties? Yes, that seems sensible. Not that anyone would credit you to be my sister, Mary does not have your striking colouring."

"No." She hesitated and then went on in a spirit of full disclosure, "The Doctor misunderstood and took me for your wife. I — I didn't contradict him, I'm sorry. In- in the kerfuffle it seemed a pointless complication to explain." She was scarlet by now but he seemed unperturbed.

"Yes probably." He frowned looking round the room. "I assume that there is a male attendant of some kind in the house?"

"My coachman Bob has been helping me to watch you, why?" she asked, perceiving a certain agitation. Had he realised he was naked and wondered who had undressed him?

He looked relieved. "Could you send him up? I ah -" he stopped, and she watched him go slowly pink "I need to -" he waved his hand lower and comprehension dawned on her as she realised the poor man had been in bed for close to fifteen hours without relieving himself.

Suppressing a nervous giggle, she nodded feeling her own face flush. "Of course! I'll fetch him, and perhaps you would like something to eat?"

"Yes, probably. Thank you," he said watching her leave the room.

His Lordship, left alone with his bursting bladder stared at the ceiling and tried to piece together the last twenty-four hours of his life. Bits of it appeared to be missing. His head ached abominably and between that and his bladder and his uneasy stomach, he felt at a distinct disadvantage in trying to think clearly.

The door opened and a middle-aged man of solid body and friendly face came in carrying a bottle, an instrument his lordship was very pleased to see.

"Miss Anne told me you was in need of a leak your Lordship. I thought this might do you, seeing as how you can't be getting up just yet." He lifted the coverlets and offered his lordship the bottle which he took gratefully. Having arranged it appropriately Denzil closed his eyes in deep relief.

Handing the bottle back he said, "Thank you! Very much!"

"My pleasure Sir. Bob Newell's the name, pleased to be of service."

"Delighted Bob. I gather you undressed me?"

"I did that me Lord. And ah," Bob coughed "You don't need to worry about any gossip in regard to Miss Anne me Lord, not from me, nor the post-boys neither. They been told to keep their chamfers closed, or I'll pound their daylights for 'em. Miss Anne's as good as ever twanged Sir, I won't brook no harm to her in anyways, if you take my drift!" said Bob with a meaningful look.

"I do Bob, and you can rest assured no harm will come to Miss Harcourt from me either," responded Denzil quickly.

Bob, who had adopted the air of a pugnacious bulldog in defence of a bone, seemed satisfied by this. "Well, I'll just empty this and put it by the bed, so you can reach it when you need."

Just then the door opened and Anne came in followed by a strapping lass with red cheeks and an ample bosom, bearing a tray laden down with bowls and platters. Bob slipped out with his bottle while the girl laid down the tray and Anne came towards him saying, "Gail has brought your lunch, and I am going to feed you since you are not advised to sit up."

Denzil eyed Gail and the tray with wary fascination and said faintly, "Thank you. I fear I'm not up to a meal of those proportions yet."

Anne said comfortably "Don't worry some of it is for me. I haven't had my lunch yet either."

"Ma is in discussions with Mr Fenton about his turkey, do you think his lordship might fancy a bit of turkey meat your ladyship?" asked Gail as she arranged a napkin over his Lordships stomach and addressed Anne over his head.

Anne flushed slightly and said carefully, "Would you fancy some turkey Denzil?"

I would never run from you Denzil. Had he dreamt that?

"Ah please don't go to any bother for me," he said hastily.

"No bother!" said Gail. "He's a young'un, so he shouldn't eat tough. And when we're done with him, there's Mrs Pots's Piglet's. We won't run out of vittles, snow, or no snow! Fenton's a nip farthing but Ma's got his measure and won't be diddled, no how. Not even for an Earl," said Gail closing the door behind her.

Denzil dragged his eyes from the door back to Anne who had dissolved into laughter on the bedside chair. "What" he asked faintly, is so funny?"

"Your face!" she said giggling helplessly. "Not even for an — an Earl!" she choked. Gasping she said, "I'm sorry I was obliged to puff off your consequence a bit as Mrs Kennedy was inclined at first to cast us back out into the snow when we arrived, with you all covered in blood and snowflakes. It was why I had to tell her I was Lady Mary. I hope you don't mind me calling you Denzil just now -"

"I don't mind at all." He reached out his hand and took hers "I think I may owe you my life Miss Harcourt. If you hadn't come across me in the snow, I may well have frozen to death."

She shuddered and squeezed his hand. "I know I've been saying prayers of gratitude ever since I found you that we came upon you when we did. Bob said he almost ran over you, you were half buried in snow."

"Very fortunate. Your Coachman is very protective of you by the way. He as good as told me he would thump the living daylights out of me if you came to any hurt through my agency. I am glad you have such loyal servants about you Miss Harcourt."

She flushed. "He didn't? How dare he! As if you would -" she gasped and stopped. "I mean, yes, he is very protective. He put me on my first pony you know."

"I know perfectly how it is. My groom taught me to ride when I was in short coats and frequently forgets that I have been out of them for years!" He smiled and drew an answering smile from her which made her face light up. "We must have met in London, why don't I remember you?"

She extricated her hand from his and stood up turning towards the tray. "Yes, we did meet, my Lord, but it was some years ago. I have lived quite retired for many years now. I keep house for my brother." She removed the covers and came back to the bed with a steaming bowl and a spoon. Seating herself she said, "Now would you like a little of this chicken soup?"

"I suppose I should eat something, though I'm liable to choke in this position." He said. "I feel quite helpless like this, it's not a comfortable feeling."

She set the bowl and spoon down on the bedside table and bent over him carefully raising his head gently with an additional pillow. "Is that better?"

"Yes, I think so. Thank you." He watched her pick up the bowl and spoon again and reseat herself prepared to spoon-feed him. "You are most kind, Miss Harcourt."

She offered him a spoonful of the soup which he took. It was hot and salty, and the first nourishment he had had since break-fast the previous day. As it hit his stomach, he realised that he was hungry after all.

Spooning in the soup she said carefully, "For the sake of our deception you should probably call me Mary, you know." "Thank you, Mary," he said meekly, accepting another mouthful of soup.

By the time they had worked their way through most of the contents of the tray, Bob came back with the bottle which he stowed discretely and Anne left him in peace to sleep.

CHAPTER 17

*J*ack and Timothy arrived at Seven Oaks close on seven in the morning and were greeted by Mary in her night cap and winter dressing gown. Mary flung herself on her husband's chest, sobbing with relief and recoiled moments later. "Timothy you're soaked to the skin!" Her spouse, whose nose was red as a berry, opened his mouth to reply and sneezed instead.

Sending servants scuttling to fill a hot tub, Mary, made to hustle Timothy upstairs and turned back to hug Jack quickly. "Jack! I am so glad you came. Viviana's uncle sent a note indicating that Viviana is not with them! I am distracted. No word from either of them and the snow building up! What shall we do?"

Jack hugged her. "Go see to Timothy, he's frozen solid.

Hardy and I will ask around, find out what we can."

"At this time of night? You're sodden too –"

"I've been in the Peninsular Mair, this is nothing. I'll be fine. Hardy can do for me."

With a hand to her head and muttering things about hot mustard plasters, Mary ran up the stairs. Jack turned to Hardy who had followed him into the hall with his baggage and signalled him to follow him up the stairs to his room.

An hour later dressed in clean, dry clothes Jack met Hardy in the stables to compare notes on what they had each discovered. Jack had searched the house and sent Hardy below stairs to discover what the servants knew.

Jack entered the stables to find Hardy sitting on a bale of hay beside a young woman in a mob cap. She was huddled in a cloak, beneath which the hem of her night gown could be seen. She was red-eyed and snuffling into a large blue handkerchief that Jack recognised as belonging to Hardy. Hardy was speaking, "Now don't take on Lily, I don't hold with hurtin' wimmen and neither does the captain. You tell him the truth and naught will come of it see if I'm right."

"What's to do Hardy?" said Jack coming to a halt in front of the pair.

"Lily's the second chambermaid Captain. She's got summat to tell you," said Hardy with an encouraging pat to Lily's quaking shoulders.

Jack squatted down so that he could see Lily's face and said gently, "What is it? Don't be afraid, just tell me what you know, people's lives may be at stake here. It's important."

Lily dropped her hands to her lap and wrung the handkerchief. "I wouldn't have done it, only he offered me a sovereign Sir and another if I brought him information regular!" she said in a rush.

"Who Lily?"

"I don't know his name Sir, but he were a gentleman by his dress and manner. At first, I thought he wanted — well you know Sir –" She blushed and looked sideways at Hardy. "But I'm a good girl, my ma'am taught me proper and I weren't having none of that!"

Jack's lips twitched as Hardy flushed in the light from the lamp hanging from the rafters above their heads. So, Lily was the country housemaid Hardy had been flirting with? He transferred his attention back to Lily patiently. "I see. So, what did he want?"

"I told you Sir!" she said "Information! About Miss Torrington."

Jack's pulse skipped a beat and thumped heavily "Go on. What did you tell him?"

She flushed then and looked down "Just where Miss Torrington went, and what she did. Her Abigail is a bit of a natterer, so it wasn't hard to find out. And a Sovereign's a lot of money, Sir. Our Bertram's got a bad foot, the money will help him get proper doctorin'!" she added with a show of spirit.

"And when did you last speak to this gentleman?" asked Jack grimly.

"Yesterday morning. It were after Miss Torrington went riding with his Lordship." Lily swallowed and went on "I was upstairs when Miss Torrington and his Lordship came back from riding, and she was in one her tempers. His Lordship tried to reason with her, but she weren't havin' any. He chased her up the stairs, and she slammed the door in his face. I was standing behind the hall curtain and quaking in my shoes lest he discover me!"

"They quarrelled, did they?" Jack asked sitting back on his haunches, his heart thumping harder. God, what happened after he left? "What happened then?"

"His Lordship went back to his study and Miss Torrington stayed in her room for a bit. I don't know what happened then because I had to go below stairs and Mrs Madding had me clean all the silver. It was after eleven when his Lordship discovered she was missing. No closer to twelve! That was when the *other* gentleman came to call."

"Harcourt?" asked Jack sharply.

Lily nodded her head miserably and started to weep again "I'm going to lose my situation, aren't I? I'm so sorry Sir. I know I shouldn't ha dun it, but…."

Jack was frowning ferociously and cut across her blubbering. "No, you shouldn't, and I hope it's a lesson to you! If harm has come to Miss Torrington or my brother because of it–!"

He stopped and took a breath as she sobbed harder, burying her face in the handkerchief. "Answer me one more question." He stood up and paced a bit as Lily's sobs bordered on hysterical. "Lily! Listen to me." He turned and came back her and said more gently, "It's all right Lily. You won't lose your situation if you answer me truthfully and promise never to do anything so wrong and foolish ever again. Now stop crying Lily and listen to me."

Lily made a valiant effort to stop her flood of tears and sat up gulping "I — I p-promise! I won't never. I'm that sorry –"

"All right Lily, now tell me everything you know about this gentleman who paid you to spy in Miss Torrington. Where did you meet, how many times did you see him, what he said to you and what he looked like. Everything. Slowly from the beginning."

When he had Lily's whole story, Jack left her sodden and repentant with Hardy, telling him to saddle two horses, re pack overnight bags for them both and meet him round the front in half an hour. Hardy nodded and Jack and went back to the house.

RUNNING up the stairs he made his way to Mary's room and tapped on the door. Mary opened it and said softly "Jack! What are you doing?"

"I'm leaving in half an hour as soon as Hardy has the horses saddled. Is Timothy awake can I speak with him?" he pushed past her as he spoke, going into the room where he found his brother-in-law huddled under the blankets shivering and sneezing.

"Tim!"

Wroxton opened one eye and said thickly, "Sorry Jack I seem to hab caught a chill! Ahchoo!" he sneezed hard and Mary came forward twittering with concern.

"Where is Harcourt's country house? Do you know?"

Blowing his nose, Timothy squinted at him. "Ranald's estate is in Cambridgeshire."

"No, the grandson, does he have a property?"

Mary broke in. "Jack what are you talking about? What has Harcourt got to do with this?"

Jack ignored her. "Think, Tim, it's important!"

Wroxton cleared his throat and Mary answered for him. "He has a house in Hertfordshire, near Rush Green. His sister keeps it for him. Poor thing, she never took and after one season she retired to keep house for him. I haven't seen her in years — Anne, that was her name. She was cursed with the Harcourt red hair. Don't you remember Timothy?"

Wroxton closed his eyes and Jack said, "Never mind his housekeeper! Do you have any more precise directions than that?"

Mary shook her head and Jack turned to leave.

"Jack wait! Where are you going?"

He turned back gave her a quick peck on the cheek. "After Harcourt," he said as he headed for the stairs.

Following him Mary said, "But why? You can't go out now! You've been riding all night, it's snowing, the roads are all but impassable!"

Jack ran down the stairs saying, "If I'm right, Harcourt has her, and Den too for all I know!"

"Then she is ruined Jack! What can you do?"

"Kill Harcourt!" he snapped and grabbing his great coat,

left the house to Mary's wail of distress. Jack ran down the steps to Hardy waiting out the front where he had two horses with saddle packs on their rumps, stamping and blowing in the cold night air. It was still snowing and the light was poor due to the heavy clouds.

Jack donned his great coat and checked the girths on the stallion. It was Tempest, and he was lifting his head and making his displeasure at this dawn jaunt known. Hardy was standing by his head. "He's fresh Captain. If he don't throw you into a snow drift, he'll be good for several hours hard ride I should think."

"Thank you, Hardy. Is Lily all right?"

"She'll do." Hardy handed him Tempest's bridle and went to the second horse, Redmund. In bright sunlight his coat shone red as shame. He was a hand shy of Tempest's height, and a good deal better tempered. "I suppose it'd be a waste of breath to say we should wait till the snow stops?"

"Yes" said Jack tersely.

Hardy shrugged and prepared to mount. His foot was in the stirrup as Jack mounted Tempest and swinging the stallion round said "I'm for Rush Green. You take the London Road towards Belmont. I want you to find his Lordship and tell him I'll bring Miss Torrington back."

"You're never going to tackle that blackguard on your own Captain!" said Hardy missing his step and trying again for the stirrup. Levering himself into the saddle, he wheeled his horse to follow Jack, who was already trotting down the drive.

"I have my pistols Hardy. Tell my brother not to worry," said Jack over his shoulder.

Hardy caught him up at the gate, "Oh surely! His Lordship won't worry knowin' that!"

CHAPTER 18

*V*iviana allowed her host to help her descend from the coach and lead her over the threshold of what he assured her was now her new home. Stiff and cold from the long ride in the carriage Viviana was glad of the huge fire in the room he led her to. Even lit by several candelabra the room was dark with wood grain panelling and the furniture heavy with worn upholstery. Above the fireplace were a crossed pair of duelling swords. Anthony sent servants scuttling to provide refreshment and told her to make herself comfortable. He then left her standing by the fire to contemplate her fate.

She stared around while her feet slowly thawed, looking for some opportunity, something to save herself. She had contemplated seizing the pistol in the drawer under the coaches forward seat. But had been afraid it was un-loaded. If it was and he knew it, she would risk antagonising him to no purpose. She looked at the duelling foils and wondered.

Anthony re-entered the room a few minutes later to find her still standing by the fire. She looked at the frown on his face. "What is it?"

"I left instructions for the local vicar to be here when I

arrived, but it seems the damned fellow has taken himself off elsewhere. Something about a funeral."

"Anthony, I cannot stay here without a skerrick of a chaperone if we are not to be married at once-" she said allowing a note of panic to enter her voice. Best to let him think she was resigned to her fate.

His eyes narrowed. "Do you think I have brought you here under false pretences my dear? I assure you it is not the case and I will find a vicar to marry us, never fear! I am as eager to tie the knot as you are." He reached for her hand and kissed it. She let him and then withdrew it gently.

"Then what are we to do."

"Nothing tonight my love. It is a pity my sister is not here, she would have been a more than adequate chaperone, alas she is visiting our grandfather in Cambridgeshire. However, I daresay we will make shift without her. She had been my chatelaine forever you see and had the ordering of the house, but you needn't fear she will be underfoot once we are married. She has already made arrangements to go and live with a friend in Bath."

Viviana digested this information in silence and then gathering her scattered wits said, "Anthony it is most awkward, but I have no clothes with me –"

"Ah that is all taken care my love. I hope you will approve my taste. You will find everything you desire in your room. Come I will show you."

She stepped back and lifting her left hand from behind the folds of her cloak she revealed the duelling foil. "No Anthony. This has gone far enough. Fetch a vicar or let me go. I will not allow you to ruin me!"

He stared at the foil that she was pointing at his chest, and slowly he smiled. "My dear this is quite unnecessary. Put it down before you hurt yourself."

She ignored this, keeping the foil trained on him. It was a light instrument with a fine point. She had checked, it was sharp enough for her purpose. "I am in deadly earnest Anthony. I will not allow you to ruin me. Come a step closer and I *will* hurt you!"

He stared at her dumbfounded and made a discovery, "You are left-handed?"

She nodded. "I write with my right hand, but I learned to fence with my left hand."

"Good God. Does Stanton know you fence?"

"No."

"Were you planning on telling him?"

She smiled and shook back her hair from her face "After we were married, I planned to confess to all my sins."

He laughed. "My dear you would have been bored to tears with Stanton inside of a month! And you would be wasted on him. He would abhor all you best attributes!"

"Oh, not all of them," she responded recalling some heated kisses. Stanton was not the cold fish Harcourt thought him to be, she could attest to that. But he didn't, she had to admit, compare to Jack who had never kissed her at all.

He laughed again and attempted to step forward and was brought up short by the point of the rapier. "That is my father's duelling sword, you realise that don't you?' he said conversationally. "He killed at least two men with it, I believe."

"How many have you killed?" she asked, taking a firmer grip on the hilt of the sword.

"Four, no I tell a lie, five. Three with pistols. Only two with the blade I fear." His eyes narrowed and he said, "Do you wish to test me my dear?"

She swallowed. He was bigger, heavier and by far stronger than she. It would not be an even match, but she had the advantage of being very light on her feet and she was quick. She also hoped that he would underestimate her. She nodded. "Very well. If I win you will let me go."

He smiled with amusement. "And if you lose you agree to

marry me as soon as I can find a wretched clergyman to perform that office for us?"

She swallowed, "I want your word as a gentleman!"

"No, my dear, I'll not wager you." He moved towards her and raised the blade threateningly.

"I mean it Anthony, I will fight you to the death if necessary!"

"Good God!" he said as her blade brought him up short. This was a desperate gamble, could she win?

Seeing that she was in deadly earnest he grinned. "This won't last long my dear."

She circled away from him so that he could reach down the other sword. She wondered that he hadn't noticed that one was missing. But then he had been preoccupied. He moved the furniture out of the way to clear a space in the centre of the room, and he took off his coat, rolling up the sleeves of his shirt and removing his cravat. His shirt collar revealed the solid column of his neck and a hint of the hairs on his chest. Without his coat, his chest and shoulders showed solid and muscular through the fine linen of his shirt. She put down her rapier and removed her cloak, keeping a careful eye on him. He looked at her gown. "You can hardly fight in petticoats, you'll trip!"

She stripped swiftly to her chemise and turned to face him, her sword held, engarde.

He stared at her fascinated, his sword pointed down. "My dear, Stanton could never handle you!"

She feinted. "Put your sword up Anthony!"

He raised his blade, and they saluted with a quick clash of metal on metal. She moved lightly on her feet, attacking with swift and deadly aim; he recovered from his surprise and moved rapidly to block her attack. She had to strike quickly or she would lose. His strength and stamina would win out over her speed in short order. She feinted high and with a flick of her wrist came in low, but frustratingly his sword was there to sheer hers away uselessly. Her wrist ached. He was fighting her with his right hand, which was awkward and with a quick change he swapped to his left hand to match her, changing the balance.

It threw her momentarily and she moved back, trying to recover her advantage. She shifted sideways to give him less of a target. Sweat bloomed on her face and body and her palm felt slippery, her breath came in gasps, her upper arm was truly aching now. She couldn't last much longer. He was barely showing any signs of effort, and she concluded that he wasn't really trying yet. She pressed back into the fray, desperately looking for an opportunity, some weakness to exploit.

For the first time he began to attack, and she was flung onto the defensive, desperately parrying his thrust with her blade. If he used his full strength on her now, he could disarm her in seconds. She had to find an opening! She flicked her wrist, releasing the clashed blades and thrust with all her body weight, aiming for his belly. His sword was there and flicked her blade up, but he must have missed his footing on the edge of the carpet, because he lost his balance momentarily, staggering, and her blade came free and kept going, slicing upwards into his shoulder where it stuck, quivering.

She yanked it free and a cry was surprised out of him, his blade fell, nerveless from his hand. Blood bloomed on his shirt and he stared down at it. She dropped her blade and sank to her knees sobbing for breath.

"The Devil!" he said faintly and staggered backwards into a chair. He put his hand to the wound bringing it away blood smeared. "You couldn't have done that if I hadn't tripped!" he said hoarsely. He shook his head as if having difficulty focusing.

She was scrambling into her clothes and struggling to re-lace her gown. He rose to his feet and shuffled towards her as if his legs had forgotten how to work. Had she hit some vital spot? Her fingers were shaking so hard she fumbled with the buttons and laces. He reached for her and she moved away. "I'm going Anthony, unless you want me to kill you outright?"

He laughed. "You haven't the stomach for that!"

"Don't test me!" she said pulling her laces tight.

"I never expected you to hit me!" he confessed, pulling her in with his right arm, the left hung uselessly at his side. She pushed against his chest but he his arm was an iron bar, and she realised how little strength he had exerted against her in the fight. He was swaying slightly, and she wondered if she had hit a vital spot after all. Blood had soaked his left sleeve and was running down his arm dripping onto the carpet. The metallic, meaty tang of it caught in her throat and made her want to retch. She swallowed.

"Let me go Anthony!"

"Never!" he said hoarsely. "I have been too gentle with you!" he grabbed the back of her skull in his right hand and forced her head up, his thumb and fingers squeezing just below her ears. It hurt and made her vision blur. He kissed her roughly, forcing her lips apart with his tongue.

Gagging she struggled, grabbed his injured shoulder and squeezed with her fingers. At the same time, she brought her knee up and aiming true, got him neatly between the legs. He let her go abruptly with an oomph! of pain and staggered backwards, tripped over an occasional table, and fell heavily. Her fingers were dripping blood, and she was panting with fear and rage.

His body lay still and she bent over him. Had she killed him? His eyes were closed and his face was ashen pale. She felt for a pulse in his neck and found it. He was unconscious not dead. She looked at the occasional table and realised he must have hit his head on the edge of it as he fell. She let out a sob with sudden relief, sinking to her knees on the bloodied carpet.

CHAPTER 19

*A*nne poked her head in the door of Denzil's room, to find him awake staring at the wall. Seeing her he said relieved, "At last! I am bored to tears lying here. Please will you bear me company?"

She coloured and came into the room closing the curtains over the window and then turning her attention to the fire. "Of course, if you wish. I came to see if you wished to eat, it is lunchtime."

"Is it? It seems hardly any time since breakfast. What I would like is to sit up, and perhaps a drink."

She came to his bedside and assisted him to sit up. "How is your head?" she asked anxiously.

"Much better." he accepted a glass of barely water from her. "Thank you." he let out a breath and confessed, "I am trying to piece together what happened, but I seem to be missing something."

She sat folding her hands in her lap. "Perhaps if you tell me what you remember, the effort of recall will jog your memory?" she said helpfully.

"You are a very rational woman, Miss Harcourt," he said

running his eyes over her in appreciation. Now that he had the leisure to look, he took in the details of her appearance and noted several things that he had been too dazed earlier to notice. She had the greenest eyes he had ever seen, with absurdly long dark lashes and nicely arched eyebrows, her features were too strong to fit the mode of delicate prettiness that was the fashion, but she struck him suddenly as quite beautiful, in an unusual and arresting fashion.

"How the devil did you manage to escape matrimony, Miss Harcourt?" he said, quite forgetting what he had been going to say.

She flushed scarlet and a said repressively, "I only had one London season, and I didn't take!"

"I find that difficult to believe," he said observing the blush which left her cheeks with a rosy glow and made her eyes shine. "No offers at all?"

"This is hardly a proper conversation for us to be having, Lord Stanton," she said sharply.

"You're right it isn't. I apologise. I didn't mean to offend you." She had turned her head away and appeared to be biting her lip, in an attempt to cajole her, he said impulsively "I was carried away by your eyes!"

She jerked her head back towards him, and he watched her struggle with herself between indignation and laughter. "Denzil you're flirting with me, stop it!"

He laughed which made his head hurt, but he didn't mind, her eyes were glowing. "Not at all, I was merely being truthful. Which you were not. Confess you received several offers and refused all of them, why?"

She veiled her eyes. "I received no offers."

"Forgive my selfishness, but I'm glad you did not, or you wouldn't be here now, and I might be dead." He was feeling unaccountably giddy, it must be the blow to his head. It had addled his brain considerably.

"Don't say that!" she said sharply, and he caught the stricken look in her eyes before she veiled them and went on with an attempt at lightness, "You were going to relay the events of the past twenty-four hours as you remember them -"

That look had jolted him. They were virtual strangers to one another, and yet she looked as if the idea of his death would break her heart. How could such a delightful woman be related to that devil Harcourt? With the thought a number of things that had been fizzing round the back of his brain fell into place.

"Good God!"

He was hardly aware that he had spoken aloud, but she leaned forward. "You have remembered something?"

HE WAS LOOKING at her as if he had recalled something distinctly unpleasant and her heart skipped a beat. He looked quite pale, and she wondered what could have occurred to make him look so ill suddenly.

"Yes, I have and very perturbed to find myself caught by the heels in this regard," he replied cryptically. "Good god what am I going to do?"

"Can I help?" she asked anxiously, reaching for his hand on the coverlet.

He let her take it with a distracted air and squeezed it absently. "You are most kind, but I don't know that there is anything you can do. Except — you wouldn't know your brother's whereabouts or intentions, would you?"

"Anthony? No. He left my grandfather's house before I did, quite early I believe. I gathered the impression that he was going to stay with a friend. He didn't tell me his direction, why?"

"He called upon me just before — Damn!" seeming to recall his company he said, "My apologies Miss Harcourt, but I am most over set. I fear that -" he stopped, his eyes fixed on the window over her shoulder.

"You need not apologise, I have heard far worse. My brother is not wont to hide his tongue in my presence."

As if rousing himself he said, "Well his lack of conduct is no excuse for mine."

She pressed his hand earnestly. "Please tell me what is troubling you, perhaps I can help. What has my disreputable brother done?"

"I fear -" He stopped and then went on. "I regret to say this, and I fervently hope that I am mistaken, but I fear that he may be bent on doing someone I — I care for harm."

"Very likely," said Anne flatly.

"Good heavens, you mean that you are not surprised?"

"Not in the least. Anthony is always strongly desirous of getting his own way and I regret to say it, usually he does get it. So, if someone is foolish enough to thwart him, he is quite capable of doing them serious damage," replied Anne frankly.

"You are not fond of your brother ma'am?"

"I loathe him!" said Anne vehemently. "In fact, I am very glad that he has decided to marry, although I feel sorry for his poor wife, but at least it will relieve me of a duty that has been burdensome for many years!" said Anne swallowing a sob.

He turned his head quickly on the pillow which made him wince. "He told you that he intends to marry.? Did he say who -"

"No, he didn't deign to tell me the name of the woman unfortunate enough to accept him, he simply informed me that my services were no longer required and that I should look elsewhere for accommodation!" said Anne, hunting furiously for a handkerchief.

"You mean that he would throw you out into the street? Surely not -" He appeared stunned by such a lack of family feeling.

Anne, who had found her handkerchief, blew her nose sharply. "Oh, do not concern yourself, I will do very well. I intend to pretend I am a widow and seek a situation. I assure you that, despite my brothers' strictures on the subject, I am quite a competent housekeeper!"

"Anne you can't!" he said clearly horrified.

She got up and paced to the window too agitated to remain seated. "What choice do I have! Oh, I could go and keep house for Grandfather I suppose. But his temper is as bad as Anthony's, and I am rather tired of being yelled at!" she said, giving full vent to her feelings. She wiped her face and tried to stifle another sob.

"Anne come here!" he said.

She put a hand to her face, stricken. "Please — I shouldn't have said any of that. You must think me the veriest shrew! I -" She turned to go towards the door, but his voice arrested her.

"Anne! Don't leave please! Damn it I can't get out of this bed, come here!" his tone was peremptory and whether it was the habit of years to obey a command uttered with force, or some other reason, she went back to the bed and stood with one arm crossed over her stomach protectively while she blew her nose with her other hand.

Crossing both arms and hugging herself, she said, "I'm sorry. This is none of your concern. I think perhaps I haven't had enough sleep -"

He appeared distressed and perplexed. "Anne, sit down and give me your hand."

She shook her head. "I should go, you're supposed to be resting -"

"Blast it Anne, sit down!" said his Lordship losing his temper.

Anne sat.

"Thank you!" he said taking a breath and picking up her hand.

She looked down at her hand in his and her lips twitched. She glanced up at him and catching a look part way between perplexity and something that made her heart turn over, she felt a sudden burst of something that found its expression in laughter. It must have been catching because he laughed too, which made him say with a grimace, "Ow! Don't make me laugh it hurts!"

She smiled. "My brother says I am a most exasperating woman and that no man of sense would have me!"

"I think I've heard more than enough about your brother's opinions of you. I assure you that as soon as I can stand upright, I am going to take great delight in telling him so. And what's more I am going to ensure that from now on he treats you with the respect and consideration you deserve."

"I am afraid he would laugh in your face."

"That would be a grave mistake. Nothing will give me greater pleasure than teaching him better manners," said his lordship grimly.

She put a hand to her chest. "No Denzil! Anthony has already killed two men in a duel, that I am aware of, it may be more. He is equally lethal with pistols and the sword I assure you."

Stanton said quietly, "I am not one to boast Miss Harcourt, but I assure you that should it come to a contest between us, I would not lose."

"You can't know that!"

"I can and I do. Have you so little faith in me?"

"That is not the point!" she said holding his hand with both of hers.

"It is precisely the point Anne. You see me at a disadvantage at this present. But I am not such a paltry fellow as you would think me. I have seen your brother with a sword at Galliano's, believe me I can take him." He turned his hand over and squeezed hers.

She gasped. "Very well I will believe you, but please say you will not try to teach him anything... for I fear the outcome. After all, if you killed him you would have to flee the country and your family wouldn't like that. And furthermore, if you did kill him, that would leave me destitute, for the estate is entailed and every-thing would revert to Grandpapa!"

He said with a smile, "Then there is nothing for it, we will have to find you a suitable husband!"

She swallowed faintly. "Please stop funning. I told you I have no wish to marry!"

"Nonsense, every woman must wish to be married!"

She pulled her hand away sharply. "Well, I do not!"

He stared at her. *I would marry you myself except-* he broke off the thought with a sort of moan. "My brains are addled, Jack where are you when I need you?"

"Here!" said a voice at the door and Anne, who was trying to recover her complexion and her wildly beating pulse from the effects of his lordships last speech, turned to see standing in the doorway, a tall blonde man, with features similar enough to Denzil's to make her guess at the closeness of their relationship.

JACK TOOK in the sight of his brother sitting up in bed dressed only in a shirt open at the neck, with a bandage round his head and his hand in that of a strange young woman with red hair. The woman saw him looking and flushed, snatching her hand from the Earls as if caught thieving a purse. The Earl looked less perturbed and more pleased to see him. Jack was unsure what to feel or think. His overwrought emotions, which had brought him to this point in the journey were fighting for the upper hand. He shut the door behind him and strode into the room exclaiming, "Denzil, what in Hades happened to you?"

"Jack I am so glad to see you!" said Stanton putting out a hand. "As you can see, I am laid by the heels. I was set upon on the road, but what are you doing here?"

"Following you from Seven Oaks. Mary sent a letter to Wroxton begging him to come back as you had run mad and Viviana had disappeared. I was with him when the letter arrived and posted back immediately. Where in heaven's name is Viviana?"

Stanton shook his head. "I don't know, I was looking for her when this happened." He indicated his bandaged head. "I had hoped that you would know?" His eyes focused on Jacks face.

Jack felt himself flush and said tightly, "Why would I know?"

Stanton turned to the woman. "Miss Harcourt would you be so good as to look in the breast pocket of my jacket?"

Miss Harcourt? Jack goggled at the woman as she crossed the room to the wardrobe took out his brother's jacket and felt in the pockets. She produced a twist of paper. "Is this what you wanted?"

"Yes," said Stanton, holding out his hand for it. She gave it to him and put the jacket back. He then held it out to Jack. "She left me a note, you had better read it."

Jack felt his colour fade as he took the screw of paper with fingers that trembled, his heart thumped heavily in his chest. He spread the crumpled sheet and read.

My dear Denzil,

I do not expect that you will or can ever forgive me for this, but I find that I have mistaken my heart. Knowing this, I cannot go forward with our betrothal. I admit to cowardice in not telling you this face to face, as I should, and this will be just another reason for you to hate me. I am returning to my uncles' house, please inform Grandmama who will no doubt follow. I hope that while I am quite sunk below reproach, that society will not attach any blame to you for this. The failure is all mine, I do not expect that you will need to suffer the embarrassment of seeing me again.

Yours in heart break

Viviana

Jack raised his eyes to his brothers face and tried to keep his expression impassive under the question in his brothers' eyes. "What happened Jack?" asked Denzil quietly.

Jack squirmed internally but said firmly, "Nothing."

"Then why did you leave?"

Jack opened his mouth and shut it, looking down at the note

again. After a moment he turned away and paced to the fireplace, his back to the bed and his brothers' accusing eyes. He could feel them boring between his shoulder blades. He stared at the flames trying to find the right words. Finally, he said, "Nothing happened." He turned back to face Denzil. "And I left to ensure that nothing would. I told her that I esteemed her as a sister and wished her every happiness, and I meant it Den!" He took a breath. "I would never do anything so — so villainous. You know me better than that surely?"

Denzil stared at him across the room, his expression inscrutable. Eventually he said slowly, "Yes I do." His eyes dropped to his fingers pulling restlessly at the coverlet, and he let out a breath slowly though his nose. "I was sorely mistaken in her though, wasn't I?"

"Don't blame her Den! She was trying, she meant you no harm or disrespect. In fact, she told me she didn't deserve you."

"Yes, she told me that herself. I didn't understand what she meant!" said Denzil, a bitter undertone in his voice.

"I should never have come home!" said Jack wretchedly.

"Oh yes you should. Better now than later, after the wedding!" snapped Denzil. He took a breath and swallowed. "You did me a favour Jack. I'm grateful, or I will be when my pride has recovered."

"Only your pride Den? I thought you loved her?"

Denzil's mouth tightened and he said shortly, "I thought so too!"

Jack glanced at Miss Harcourt who had stood like a statue through this exchange, her eyes fixed on Denzil. *She must be Harcourt's sister? But what was she doing here with Den?*

Denzil, as if becoming aware of the trending of Jack's thoughts said, "Where are my manners. Miss Harcourt, this is my brother Captain Jack Elliot lately of the Dragoon Guards. Jack, you will be nice to Miss Harcourt, she saved my life."

Miss Harcourt blushed and disclaimed as Jack came forward

to take her hand in formal greeting. "If that is the case Miss Harcourt, then I speak on behalf of my whole family, we are most grateful." Letting go her hand he transferred his attention back to the invalid. "What happened Den? You said you were set upon, where and when?"

"Yesterday afternoon on the road to Belmont. Two men, at least I assume there were two, I only saw one, he had a gun and was on horseback. The other, I surmise, was on foot and came up behind me. He struck me a mighty blow to the back of my head, and they left me in the road, I can only assume, to perish. If Miss Harcourt had not happened along shortly thereafter, I may indeed have succumbed to the cold. I was unconscious, and by Miss Harcourt's account, partially covered in snow when she found me."

"Why did you go after her?"

"Because I was only a couple of hours behind her, I thought I could catch her, reason with her, at least find some way out of the coil that wouldn't plunge us into a major scandal. I would have caught her too if I hadn't been set upon."

"Were you robbed?"

"No, I don't believe so."

"Then what motive -?"

Denzil looked at him under his brows grimly. "I can only think of one reason -"

Jack cut across him. "Miss Harcourt I hardly like to be so importunate, but would it be possible to obtain a drink do you think?"

Miss Harcourt glanced at Denzil and back at him and inclined her head. "Of course, Captain." With a stately dignity she left the room, closing the door gently behind her.

"Jack what are you about, Miss Harcourt isn't a servant."

"I know, but I wanted to speak to you alone."

"You needn't. Miss Harcourt is fully aware of her brother's villainy."

"Is she?" Jack paced back to the bed and sat in the chair the lady had vacated. "Then it is not too much of a stretch to suggest that she may have been sent by him to delay you further!"

"What are you talking about?"

"Those men who attacked you, could one of them have been Harcourt himself?"

"Yes, I thought it likely, it's what I was going to say when you cut me off."

Jack nodded grimly. "And what is more likely then, that he sent his sister to intercept you?"

"Why would he do that?"

"He may not have wished you to die in the snow. Or perhaps he simply wished to have her find your frozen corpse and raise the alarm, I don't know. It seems mighty coincidental that she should happen along when she did."

"Nonsense. She was returning home from her grandfathers to her brother's house; Seven Oaks, lies approximately halfway between the two and Belmont is accessible from this road. I was bound to be on this route because I was going to Belmont, Viviana's Uncles house; Anne was bound to be on it on her way home."

"And she just happened to appear shortly after you were set upon? Doing it too brown Den!" said Jack noting the use of Miss Harcourt's Christian name. "I saw you holding her hand when I came in, you have been alone at this inn together since yesterday. I saw no chaperone when I came in. Are you sure you haven't been led into a mousetrap Den?"

Denzil coloured. "Of course not, what do you take me for? I've had more traps set for me than you have had hot dinners! I can assure you Miss Harcourt is not privy to her brother's dastardly plots, nor would she be inveigled into participating in them. She has far too much principle!"

Jack raised an eyebrow. "A trifle less heat Den. If you will vouch for the lady...."

160

"Yes, I do. Emphatically."

Jack sighed. "Very well, but that doesn't bring us any closer to knowing where Viviana is."

"Well, if she isn't with you then she really must have gone to Belmont. She would have reached there before nightfall yesterday."

Jack shook his head "No she didn't. Mary received a note this morning from her uncle indicating that Viviana was most definitely not at Belmont, her family was clearly still under the impression she was at Seven Oaks. It was obvious that you hadn't been at Belmont either, so I set out on this road to find both of you!"

"If she didn't reach Belmont -"

"Harcourt!" said Jack grimly "Where precisely is his house?"

"On this road, but Anne will be able to direct you. You will go after him and bring her back?"

"Of course," said Jack, feeling murderous.

He must have looked it too because his brother said in alarm, "Jack don't call him out, it's to my account he needs to be called. Mine is the dishonour, not yours."

"You are in no fit state to prosecute your suit against him."

"Not at this moment no. But in a few days, I will be fit again -"

The door opened and Anne Harcourt came back in with a tray on which sat two pots of porter and a glass of sherry. She set the tray down and said brightly, "I felt we could all benefit from a restorative." She picked up one of the pots of porter and the glass of Sherry. She went to Denzil's other side offering the porter to him. Denzil took it with a smile.

Jack noted that it was the first time in a long while he could remember seeing his brother unshaven. He took the second pot of porter and Anne offered her glass of sherry in a toast to which both men inclined their pots and all three drank.

Lowering her empty glass Anne said firmly, "I understand Captain that you are desirous of the precise location of my brother's house?" She paused and coloured slightly "I am not in the habit of listening at doors, but your voices were raised. I would have had to be deaf not to hear you." She set the glass down on the tray. "I also understand that you may wish to hurt him? You may do so with my good will, although I would prefer it if you didn't kill him. A murder in the family would not be pleasant for any of us."

Jack goggled at her and then looked at his brother who was grinning over his pot of porter and said sotto voce, "Superb isn't she?" He picked up her hand and kissed it. "I assure you if Jack doesn't, I will!"

Jack buried his nose in his porter and tried to sort out which way was up. Clearly the blow to his brother's head *had* addled his brain.

Anne removed her hand gently from Denzil's grasp and said quietly, "I Understand that my brother has absconded with a lady, to whom -"

"I was betrothed, yes," replied Denzil "Miss Viviana Torrington."

"Is she quite beautiful?" asked Anne wistfully.

"Yes," replied both brothers in unison.

"And is she possessed of a considerable fortune?" asked Anne.

"Yes, she is" replied Denzil.

"I see. Then naturally you will wish the captain to recover her for you with the least amount of scandal possible. You may count on me to -to provide you with whatever assistance I can." said Anne.

"You're a gem!" said Denzil reaching for her hand again.

She smiled wanly at him, evading his touch, and turned to Jack, giving him directions to Harcourt House. "It's about four hours from here." She finished.

"Do you wish me to escort you home Miss Harcourt?" asked Jack.

"Oh no!" said Anne. "I have no intention of going to Harcourt

House ever again. I shall send Bob, my coachman, to fetch my personal belongings. I shall probably go to Grandfather for a spell until I can decide what to do for the best. I may have to settle for one of my great aunts, but I do hope not, I loathe Bath and cribbage!" said Anne with a bitter edge.

CHAPTER 20

*T*he snow clouds which had been intermittent all day had cleared, leaving a velvet sky and moonlight to see by. Viviana set the tired mare to picking her way through the snow, between the trees of the estate. She was riding bareback having had neither the time nor inclination to try to find a saddle in the dark. The blood stains on her gown showed black in the eldritch light and the metallic stench caught in the back of her throat making her nauseous with fear and loathing. She hadn't killed him outright, but she had left him to bleed to death on the carpet, unless one of the servants found him. *Which they would surely?*

Viviana pushed the thought away and tried to focus on her direction. Was she going the right way to find the road? The moonlight reflected brightly off the snow but the corresponding shadows among the trees up ahead were dark as pitch. She shivered inside her cloak, cold, tired, hungry, and more than a little bit frightened. With only had the haziest idea where she was and the further, lady penetrated into these trees the more she feared she was lost.

Panic nibbled at her, she shook her head to dislodge it,

164

leaning forward to pat the mare comfortingly. Lady shook her head and snorted, picking her feet up fastidiously. "I'm sorry" murmured Viviana looking about her and straining her eyes in the dark. *Which way to go? Where was the road from here?* She thought she should have come to it be now. *Perhaps they had got turned around in her panic to get away from the house?*

The snow blanketed ground seemed to muffle sound making her feel as if she and Lady were the only creatures awake in the tree dotted landscape. As they moved cautiously forward, the trees occasionally obscured the sky above, plunging them into shadow. She shivered again as snow, dislodged by her passing beneath a branch, rattled off the canopy and plopped onto her cloak. A few flakes, caked icily together, got inside the collar of her cloak, and ran down her back making her utter a tiny shriek and shudder convulsively. The mare, already spooked, started, and kicked out making her clutch the horse's mane and clench with her knees to stay on, bending further forward over her withers.

It was then that she heard the first yelp and call of the dogs. Her heart thumped wildly as she listened with straining ears to the baying of the hounds and the unmistakable sounds of pursuit. It was distorted by the trees and the snow, such that, she couldn't tell which direction it was coming from. She felt Lady trembling, her ears twitching madly.

She urged her mount forward, weaving amongst the trees, trying to keep the sound behind her, but not sure that she was succeeding. Her breath rasped in her throat, the cold air making it ache. She pushed the tired horse to go faster, the panic she had been holding at bay, feathered upwards and exploded as the sounds of the pack behind her got louder and closer. This was reminiscent of the chase down the London Road that morning, was it only that morning? It seemed an aeon ago. But that had been in broad daylight on a paved road, albeit one covered in snow. This was different and several degrees more terrifying.

The lower branches of trees scraped at her and dumped snow on her as the horse pelted forward through the thickening forest, trying to put distance between them and the increasingly frenzied pursuit. She clung to the mare as she urged her forward, dodging between patches of moonlight and darkness, the cold air buffeting her face and searing her lungs.

An excited series of barks, closer now, made her start and the horse, as if propelled by the sound, leaped forward over a snow-covered log in the path, dodged a too close tree and came a cropper on the next piece of uneven ground. The horse went down and Viviana lost her hold and was flung sideways into the bole of a tree. She hit the bark, taking the brunt of it with her back and tumbled to the ground, landing face down in icy snow.

She lay inert, as pain lanced through her chest and her lungs gasped for air, the cold seeping into her body and freezing her cheek. When she could finally move, she looked around for the mare. The sounds of the dogs were closer. She peered into the shadows and saw a dark shape on the ground, it moved as if trying to rise, and gave a pain shocked sound that split her heart.

She forced herself to her feet and staggered to where the mare lay on the ground. She touched the horse's neck and felt the pulse in it wild under her fingers. Collapsing beside the mare, she felt her legs for injury and found the damage almost immediately. Lady had broken a foreleg. Viviana felt the sobs of guilt and pain gathering under her rib cage. They forced their way up, in jagged spikes, and she sat in the snow sobbing for her poor horse and almost oblivious to the sounds of the hounds racing her down.

The first of the dogs ploughed into the place between the trees, where she lay with the horse, and yelped its frenzied acknowledgement of its find. Several more, came bounding through the snow and surrounded her, growling and snapping their teeth. Through her tears, she regarded them almost beyond terror, so battered by her emotions, that she made no effort to scramble away from them.

Hard on the heels of the dogs came Harcourt on horseback. He pulled his horse to a halt and leapt from the saddle, commanding the dogs to sit. They sat, and with only an occasional growl or wine, waited for their next orders. He took in the sight of her, half in and half out of shadow and came to kneel beside her and examine the horse.

Viviana found her voice with difficulty. "She's done for. Her leg is br-broken. Will you put her out of her misery p-please! I have no gun, or I'd do it m-myself."

He felt the broken leg gently and nodded. "Of Course. Stand back." He helped her to her feet and took a gun from the holster on his saddle. Viviana put her hand to her mouth as he took careful aim and shot the horse cleanly in the forehead. Viviana closed her eyes and sobbed, staggering a bit on the uneven ground. After a moment she felt him put his arm round her, and she tried to shake him off, uttering a sort of groaning protest. He ignored that and led her to his horse. "Mount."

She shook her head, resisting him, and making incoherent noises. "Do it, or I'll fling you over the saddle!" he said harshly.

She put her foot in the stirrup and allowed him to heave her up onto the saddle. He mounted behind her. Holding her with one arm round her waist, he turned the horse with his knees, and they made their way back with the dogs following.

She lay against his chest, sobbing still for her horse and hating him and herself in equal amounts. He held the reins in the hand of the arm that held her. His other arm appeared useless, his hand resting on his knee. Moving her head, she felt the sweat on his skin at the opening of his shirt. His body was hot despite the cold. Her sobs slowed, and she tried to wipe her face with her cloak. His breath was harsh in her ear and she realised that he was in considerable pain. Her movements disturbed their balance, and he gripped her more tightly with his one arm. "Don't fidget!"

She subsided too exhausted and distraught to fight back. After a bit he said roughly "Better?"

"What do you care, you monster?" she said against his good shoulder.

He laughed, but it wasn't a pleasant sound and made her shiver. "I care. You won't escape me, ladybird. I will break you to harness and when I do, you will be grateful for it."

She gasped. "Your overweening conceit is mind-boggling!
You have just killed my horse and -"

"I shot the creature at your request my dear."

"You know what I mean. You forced me to flee over rough ground in the middle of the night and that was the end result!"

"My dear you chose to flee, and you chose to put the mare at risk. Those are your decisions. I didn't make you do anything — yet! In fact, I let you put a hole in me with own fathers' duelling foil. Which makes me more of a fool than I thought myself capable of!" he snapped.

"You're impossible!" she said furiously.

"And you're not?" he asked. She put her head up to protest, and he pulled her closer with his arm an iron band round her waist and kissed her hard, bruising her lips.

She wrenched her face away. "Oh god will you stop!"

"No." She couldn't see his face at that moment because they were in shadow among the trees, but he sounded as if he was smiling. "You will have to kill me first!"

THEY EMERGED from the trees and arrived at the house a little while later, with Viviana preserving a dignified silence. He made no further attempt to kiss her. He dismounted and lifted her down with one arm round her waist. Setting her on her feet, he took her arm in a vice-like grip and dragged her up the steps to the front of the house.

He pulled her into the room they had occupied earlier, and she wrenched at his hand trying to free herself. He flung her away and sank down in a chair. She stood looking at him in the candlelight, seeing his pallor and hearing his harsh breathing.

She said in low voice, "Let me go Anthony and I won't tell anyone you were bested by a woman in a sword fight!"

He laughed which ended in a cough. "That's a hollow threat my dear. If you told that story you would be as ruined as you ever could be. You realise you have been absent from Seven Oakes for more than seventeen hours? You're ruined anyway, no one will have you, least of all the fastidious Stanton. You have the soul of a whore, and you belong with me."

"And you have the soul of a Devil! Have you no conscience?"

"Not much. And neither do you, or you wouldn't have written such drivel to Stanton and run away to his brother, you deceitful bitch. If I'm the Devil, Miss Torrington, you're more than fit to be my Mistress!"

"I should have killed you when I had the chance!"

He put his good hand to his head. "Haven't you done enough damage to me? You have cracked my skull on top of everything else. My heads like to split. Bring me a drink."

She shook her head, backing towards the door. "I'm leaving Anthony."

He raised his head and stared at her like a bloody-eyed bull. "I don't think so my dear. You won't get far on foot, and I'll just set the dogs on you again, do you fancy being dragged back here by one of them?"

She shuddered, her skin crawling at the look in his eyes.

"You wouldn't."

"I'm running out of patience, try me!" She swallowed.

"I didn't think so," he said softly. "Now fetch me a drink; and then you're going to help me upstairs to bed, like a good wife!"

On legs gone to jelly from reaction and fear, she crossed the room to the sideboard and poured him a generous measure of brandy from the decanter. She proffered the glass and he took it, toasting her silently with it. He tossed it back and held it out for a refill. She repeated the action, and he drank half of it and eyed her over the rim of the crystal cut glass. Some of his colour was returning. He said huskily, "Have some yourself, you look like you need it."

A bubble of laughter came up out of nowhere then, and she gasped, thinking that she must look a complete wreck, with her hair in a tousled disgrace, her dress ill-laced, blood on her skirt and hands, and her dress and cloak dripping with melted snow. Her instinct to refuse the drink, was overborne by that sudden, irrational impetus to recklessness, that possessed her at odd moments. Removing her cloak and letting it fall at her feet, she seized the glass from him and drained it. She choked on the strong liquor as it burned her throat then settled in her stomach with a comforting warmth.

He rose slowly from the chair. "Come. You can attend to my wounds properly above stairs and show me some wifely concern now that you have done trying to kill me."

She set the glass on the table. "How do you know I don't mean to smother you in your sleep?"

His face grimaced in a half smile. "I'll take my chances. I don't believe you're capable of murder."

"Don't you?" she had moved to his right side and took his arm.

He looked down at her. "Not like that any way. I think you could have stuck that blade in me somewhere fatal, but I don't think your intention was to kill me."

They had reached the door and she said, "True. My intent was to disable you."

"Well, you have done that. Let that content you."

"But you have reneged on your word," she said as they crossed the hall to the foot of the newel staircase.

They ascended the stairs slowly as he said, "I never gave you my word. You made a mistake my dear if you assumed that I am a gentleman of honour. I am no more that, than you are a lady of virtue. We are a well-matched pair."

They reached the landing and ascended to the second floor, before she replied. "My virtue is still intact Sir."

"Not for much longer."

They reached his bedchamber door, and he put out his good arm to open the door for her. With a gentle shove to her lower back, he pushed her over the threshold and closed the door behind them.

CHAPTER 21

*L*eft alone with the Earl once more, Anne became busy tidying the room, making up the fire and trimming the lamps, the afternoon was drawing in already. She was conscious of Denzil's silence and glanced discreetly at him from time to time. He seemed caught up in a brown study which made her heart sink. She itched to know what that note had said, but the captain had either taken it with him, or dropped it in the fire. She was stunned to gather that any woman fortunate enough to find herself betrothed to Denzil could jilt him. It gave her a very odd idea of Miss Torrington.

She sat back on her heels staring at the flames in the fireplace thoughtfully. "Do you suspect that my brother has something to do with Miss Torrington's disappearance?"

"How much did you overhear?"

"Quite a bit," she admitted.

He sighed, and she looked round at him from her place by the hearth. "Yes, I suspect precisely that," he said. "It was your brother that found Miss Torrington's note. It had fallen into the coal scuttle, or at least that is where he produced it from."

She rose and walked slowly across the room, piecing things together in her mind. "Do you think he planned this?"

He shrugged. "I don't see how. He could not have predicted that Miss Torrington would flee my house yesterday."

"Could he not? What if he engineered it?"

"How could he have done that? He hasn't seen her since he was in London, well before Christmas."

"Hasn't he?" she asked.

"No, of course not. Miss Torrington has been staying at Seven Oaks since two weeks before Christmas."

"You are probably right," she said softly.

"What makes you think he could have seen her?" She shook her head. "Nothing, I dare say you are right-"

"But-?" he prompted her.

"My brother told me quite definitely that he planned to be married." She coloured and went on, "He quarrelled with my grandfather over it. At least I think that was why they fell out again at Christmas. It was an unpleasant sojourn. My brother and Grandpapa do not get on. I hate quarrelling and loud voices. And both of them seem to take such pleasure in being in a pelter! It makes me shake in my boots!" she sat down in the chair by the bed and pulled a face. "I'm a very poor honey when It comes to loud voices!"

"Most understandable," responded his Lordship soothingly.

"Well yes, but what has me in a puzzle is how Anthony could be so certain he was to be married, if his object was to marry Miss Torrington, and she was engaged to you."

"Are you certain that the lady he intended to wed was Miss Torrington?"

"No, I am not. You would have a better idea of that than I. Was there any lady he was paying particular attention to in London?" she asked.

Denzil nodded. "Miss Torrington. He was one of her most persistent suitors."

"And did she show a partiality for him?"

He pursed his lips ruefully. "Well earlier in the piece she did, but you see I was under impression that in the end she preferred me to him. She did accept my proposal."

Anne pleated the folds of her gown carefully. "I see." She paused and finally said awkwardly "My brother has done some — quite wicked things in the past, but none so heinous as this. I- I am at a loss to explain his behaviour on this occasion. I can only conclude that he has taken leave of his senses."

"It would seem that he was suffering from some form of delusion," responded Denzil. "But then again, it would seem, so was I."

Anne felt tears of sympathy start to her eyes and tried to wipe them surreptitiously. He caught her hand. "Why are you crying?"

She shook her head. "Foolishness! I can't bear to see you hurt and to know that my brother is the probable cause- "

"You are not responsible for your brother's actions, Anne," he said reasonably.

She sniffed. "I know, but I feel — sullied by association! I am so angry with him!"

"My dear girl, you are in no part to be associated with your brother!" he said firmly.

Anne smiled wryly. "No one has called me a girl in years Denzil. I am quite on the shelf you know."

"You will have to allow me to disagree with you on that matter," he said quietly. He was playing with her hand and meshed his fingers with hers, setting his hand palm to palm with hers. It was an intimate gesture that sent a jolt through her and altered the atmosphere between them quite suddenly. He pulled at her hand, bringing her out of her chair to sit beside him on the bed. She did it without thinking, in response to a silent command that passed between them. His eyes held hers with a look that set her pulses racing and made a pool of warmth low in her belly. She remembered peeking at his naked sleeping body and waking beside him in the early morning, full of love and longing.

Something of her thoughts must have shown in her face, for he reached out with his other arm and brought her closer. Shamelessly she offered her face for his kiss and closed her eyes as his mouth connected with hers, and she fell into a dream come true.

His mouth was warm and tender, unbearably wonderful. He disengaged their linked hands and brought her closer against his chest, deepening the kiss until she was breathless. With one hand against his chest gripping the fabric of his shirt and the other round his neck, her fingers in his hair, she responded with abandon to his kisses, losing herself in sensations she had barely dared to dream of.

The kisses went on, getting more heated, then abruptly he lifted his lips from her mouth and kissed her forehead instead, hugging her tightly. His breathing, like hers, was ragged "Anne I'm sorry -"

She whispered "Hush. It's all right. I know. Just for comfort." She buried her face in his shirt and he kissed her hair, his arms still tight around her.

He held her tightly in his arms his senses full of her scent and the soft pliable heat of her body, while his thudding heartbeat settled. *Was she right? Was it just for comfort, or something more? How could he be so in love with one woman at one moment and so overwhelmingly attracted to another in the next?* He felt so unlike himself he was badly off balance. It was alarming and exhilarating at once. He buried his face in her glorious hair and tried to think.

When he linked his hand with hers, twining their fingers, she had given him such a look there was no disguising. It had gone straight to his groin, sending a rush of heat up his body and called her to him with an irresistible force. He had never been in so much danger of behaving like a lust ridden brute in his life. Not even with Viviana had he come so close, but then he hadn't had Viviana in his arms while he lay half naked in a bed either. *Was this just a product of circumstances, over wrought emotions, rebound?*

He shifted in the bed, his groin was on fire, the temptation to throw caution to the wind and give into his baser self was so strong -

"Anne -" he loosed his hold on her and sat back against the pillows.

She raised her head from his chest and the smudged look of desire in her eyes almost undid his bid for self-control.

She sat up and touched her mouth with her fingers.

"I'm sorry -" he tried again.

She held up her hand. "Don't apologise, please!" A smile crept out and lit up her face like a candle in the dark. "No one has ever kissed me like that. I know you didn't mean anything by it. Gentlemen kiss so easily, don't they?" She turned away, standing up and moving away from the bed. She looked back at him wistfully. "I shall treasure the memory of it." She moved towards the door.

"Anne please! Don't go! It wasn't —"

She stopped, her hand on the doorknob. "What?" she glanced back at him.

He flung the bed clothes back and stood up, which made him reel a bit. She moved towards him with alarm. "Denzil be careful -!"

He regained his balance, took two strides towards her and seized her in his arms. "Be careful be damned!" he said, kissing her roughly.

She melted in his arms and kissed him back with equal fervour. He released her mouth reluctantly and rested his forehead against hers, breathing and striving for some sense of control. He could feel her hands in his hair and the sweet heat of her body pressed full length against his, a contrast with the cool air in the room, which set goosebumps on the skin of his bare legs and buttocks and across his back though the thin fabric of his shirt.

"Anne, I have never wanted a woman more than I want you right now," he admitted "But please don't run away with the notion that I am in the habit of kissing women lightly." He took a breath and moved back a fraction so that he could see her face. What he read in it made his heart turnover in a most peculiar way. No woman had ever looked at him like that before. Certainly not Viviana. Such a naked avowal of love and desire took his breath away and made his heart thump faster. *God in Heaven what had he set in train here, and what should he do?*

"It's all right Denzil, I don't expect -" she began.

"Then you should!" he cut her off. "Anne, you deserve a man who can love you with his whole heart, body, mind and soul."

She blanched and pulled away. "And you don't!" she said turning away.

"I don't know," he said helplessly. "I don't know what I'm feeling right now. But I'm experienced enough to know that lust can be deceptive. And up until two days ago I believed myself to be deeply in love with another woman. How can I know what this is, on the strength of two days acquaintance?"

She had her back to him and her voice was muffled as she said. "Of course, you can't. I don't expect — Oh blast!" she said on a sob and fled to the door, slamming it behind her.

He thought fleetingly of following her and then thought better of it. His legs felt like jelly and he felt sick to his stomach. He climbed wearily back into the bed, resting his throbbing head against the pillows and closing his eyes. His bodies lust ebbed with the removal of her presence and the resurgence to the fore-front of his mind, of all the considerations that would make giving into that lust highly inadvisable.

. . .

ANNE FLED to her bedroom and indulged in a hearty bout of tears that left her limp and sodden. She lay for a time in damp misery, the coverlet coarse and smelling of moth balls, under her cheek, but eventually she rose and washed her face and made an attempt to tidy her hair. Her body still felt heavy with frustrated desire, and her heart and her head ached in equal parts. She wondered how it could hurt so much to have her heart's desire given and then snatched away in the space of half an hour. She almost, but couldn't quite, wish that it hadn't happened.

She sat on the side of her bed and stared sightlessly at the rug, playing over in her mind what had happened. As she thought about it, she realised with a blush that she had behaved in the most abandoned way. She had wanted Denzil to kiss her so much, that, of course, he had. Men were easily led into such things. She knew that much. And even one as honourable as Denzil, could be tempted in a vulnerable moment. And he was vulnerable. He had just lost the woman he loved, been jilted in the most heartless way by a faithless whore! Anne's anger with Miss Torrington blazed up fiercely. How could she?

Anne swallowed against more tears gathering in her throat. How could anyone throw Denzil's love back in his face? It was unthinkable. Her hands clenched in her lap and she bit down on her lip until it hurt, trying to suppress another bout of weeping. She mastered the impulse and sniffed, wiping her eyes. The dear man was hurt, of course, and he turned to her for comfort because she was there. That was all it was, and she would be all kinds of a fool to think anything else.

Well, she had had her kiss and that would have to content her. But oh, how hard it was to have tasted heaven and not be allowed any more...she closed her eyes a moment, swept back in the blissful memory of his arms around her, his mouth on hers and the wonderful hard swell of his body pressed against hers. That last kiss had been fierce with passion and need. Nothing soft or gentle about it. Her body flooded with warmth, remembering, and she ached with wanting more. Lying back on the coverlet she curled round the memory and the bittersweet pain of it. Hugging it to herself as if it were a sustaining meal in a desolate landscape. Staring sightlessly at the wall, on which the shadows from the candle flame danced, she hugged her memories and fed her love starved soul.

Denzil's kisses had shattered the self-protective layers she had shrouded herself with and blown open the casing of indifference, numbness, she had been living inside of. So much feeling and emotion was overwhelming, and she felt as if she was drowning, caught in a massive wave, threatening to suck her under. It triggered a sensation of panic, and she sat up suddenly, shaking with it. A suffocating feeling in her chest made her take great gasping breaths of air, trying to shake off the feeling of dire panic.

The feeling subsided after a moment, and she got off the bed, galvanised by the desire for movement, anything to stop that dreadful sense of panic from coming back. She would go and organise his evening meal, behave as if nothing had happened. He would be relieved by her common sense, take his cue from her matter-of-fact behaviour. He couldn't, wouldn't take any foolish notions of having compromised her into his head — *would he?* She stopped with her hand on the doorknob and stared at the wood panelling.

Her heart skipped and beat a rapid tattoo against her ribs. What if he did? What if he pressed her to marry him to salvage her reputation? It would be just like him to do something ridiculously honourable like that. Could she hold out against an offer? An offer that would give her everything she wanted in one way and nothing of what she wanted in another? She swallowed. Was she strong enough to resist that kind of temptation? The thought of it made her moan out loud and clap a hand over her mouth and the other to her belly, which contracted with a pulse of longing that went straight to the place between her legs. She turned to lean against the door, hugging herself, caught in a wave of longing that took her breath away. She blinked tears from her eyes and hung onto the door until the feeling receded.

She took a breath, straightened and turned, gripped the door-knob resolutely and headed down to the kitchen to request a tray to be made up for his lordship.

~

HALF AN HOUR later she knocked on his door, armed with a dinner tray and a firm resolve.

Denzil registered the knock on the door and reached for his breeches, pulling them on he went to the door and opened it, expecting Gail or perhaps Bob.

Anne stood on the threshold bearing a tray. His heart thumped uneasily at the sight of her. Her hair was loose and slightly tousled. Did she have any idea how she looked? He stood aside to let her in, and she set the tray on the side table and said in a hearty tone that told him she was putting a brave face on things, "Are you hungry? Mrs Kennedy has prepared Mr Fenton's turkey."

"Oh," he said, not feeling hungry at all. Even in the poor lamp light he could tell she had been crying. "I'm sorry Anne. I don't think I can eat right now."

She turned away to the fireplace and busied herself with adding a log and prodding the coals into flame. He watched her rigid back and searched for something to say to break the silence. Satisfied with the fire she rose. "Shall I take it away?"

"No leave it. I may eat something later." She was avoiding his eyes and wiped her hands nervously on her gown. He was standing between her and the door. She couldn't reach it without pushing past him, and she was clearly reluctant to do so.

He put out his hand. "Anne -"

She looked at him and away. "Please don't!" she said softly.

"Don't what?" he asked, an edge of exasperation creeping into his voice.

She shook her head. "Don't apologise or — anything. I don't think I could bear that."

He stepped towards her and she shrank, which made him stop. *Damn! Was she afraid of him now?* "How can I not apologise for behaving like a brute?" he said.

She put her hands up to her face. "You didn't! It was my fault -" she said her cheeks flushing.

"Anne!" he moved and captured her hands. "My dear girl, you're shaking. Please sit down." He shepherded her to the bed, and they sat down, side by side. He retained one of her hands in his. "Anne, you have to let me make this right-"

She laughed and it had an edge to it. She shook her head. "There is no need."

"There is every need!" he insisted, gripping her hand tighter. "I lost my head" he said watching her profile. She was sitting rigidly up right, and her hand was trembling. Everything about her was repelling him as strongly as she had lured him close before. *Was this a defence or something else? Regret?*

She swallowed still not looking at him said softly, "I lost mine."

Regret. He felt a twinge of pain that had nothing to do with his head. *How had he become such a disaster with women? First Viviana and now Anne?* "I didn't mean to frighten you" he said.

She looked at him then, startled and said involuntarily,

"You didn't! I would never be afraid of you."

"But I have compromised you, allowing you to stay here quite alone with me, with no chaperone-"

"How could you have done anything else? You were out of your head for a night and bedridden for the better part of the day. If anything, I have compromised myself; and that was my choice, not yours. I could have left the servants to nurse you. I have quite selfishly abrogated that task to myself." She spoke firmly, looking him squarely in the eye as if she would make him understand something that was very important to her.

"It is hardly a selfish act," he said with a half-smile.

She ignored that and ploughed on, "And I made you kiss me!" she held up her hand when he would have interrupted and said firmly, "Yes, I did! I know how it is with gentlemen, you are — are easily led in such matters. I was overcome with sympathy for you and — and it just happened. If you had been yourself, you wouldn't have done it. Would you?" she said with something almost like a glare.

"In other circumstances I would not have used you so roughly, no," he admitted.

She swallowed and her eyes dropped, removing her hand from his grip gently she said "Well there you are then. It was my fault, and we should say nothing further on the topic." She made to rise from the bed, and he grabbed her arm.

"Anne, I will not allow you to try to bamboozle me in this way! While I regret deeply my intemperate behaviour, I do not regret kissing you. Be plain with me please, I beg. Do you regret kissing me?" He held her eyes with his and watched as they brimmed with tears.

She shook her head and her voice was husky when she spoke. "Denzil I could never regret that. But I have behaved very badly, and I would not blame you for assuming -"

"What that you are a light skirt? I know very well that you are not. I acquit you of fortune hunting too and of entrapment or any other scheme. Jack was quite convinced that your brother had sent you to trap me." He felt her start and her eyes few to his face with a look he couldn't read.

"Never!" she said in a low voice. "I wouldn't-!"

"I know, haven't I just said so?" he said touching her face lightly with his hand. "There will be the devil of a scandal when this all gets out. There is no way out of that. But I hope that the details need never be known. I have no desire for a reluctant wife and if Viviana has such a revulsion of me that she felt compelled to flee my home in the depths of a snowbound winter, I have no intention of forcing her to the altar. My only hope is that she has not met with some terrible accident or worse as a result of this intemperate start and that Jack will find her and restore her to her family unharmed." He shook his head, his face twisting with the pain he felt inside. "Hindsight is a wonderful thing is it not? I can see now how ill-suited we were, but I was blinded by an infatuation that impaired my judgement. The result is that I hardly know what to think or feel at this present. I am not accustomed to feeling so distempered."

She covered the hand resting on his knee with hers and said quietly, "I know. And for that very reason you should not regard anything that has passed between us as — as carrying more significance than — than it does."

He picked her hand up and kissed it. "Anne you are the most extraordinary woman." He hesitated, trying to think how best to phrase what he wanted to say. She had coloured at his words, but she hadn't pulled away, which was encouraging. Their knees were touching, as he held her hand and looked into her extraordinary green eyes. "I am going to sound like a cox comb now, but I think I would have to be an even greater fool, than I have already proved myself, not to realise that you have some degree of — of affection for me. Am I right?" Her colour deepened and her eyes dropped.

She nodded. "Am I so transparent?"

"Just honest, I think. Which means you deserve my honesty in return." He felt her brace herself, and went on carefully, "I don't wish to hurt you -"

She swallowed. "I know, and you shouldn't concern yourself with it. You — you didn't ask for my — my regard -"

"True, but I am not sure that it isn't the greatest gift I have ever been given. Would you consider, could you consider accepting a rather worse for wear fellow as your husband my dear?"

She blinked hard and rapidly. "Ah, Denzil don't tempt me." She took a breath and touched his face with her hand. "You are feeling battered and bruised right now, but you don't love me, and I don't think I could bear it if you didn't."

He turned his head to kiss her palm. "I think I could come to love you very much, if you would let me."

She bit her lower lip and lifted her chin slightly. "Do you? Well time will tell. We are in quite extraordinary circumstances at present. I may not appear so desirable in a more mundane setting." She took a breath and cleared her throat. "If, if you feel differently in — in a month or so, I give you leave to press your suit again. But please don't feel obliged to do so. I will not hold you to anything."

"Am not sure if that is a set down or is meant as a reprieve. But I think it that it might be a very courageous gesture" he said, reaching a tentative arm around her.

"On the contrary. It is the resolve of a complete coward," she said, letting him pull her closer.

"Well, my dearest coward, will you let me kiss you good night?" he asked softly, his mouth hovering over hers.

"Oh Denzil," she whispered, tempted beyond her strength. She let him kiss her until she couldn't think and would have lain with him there and then in the bed for all her resolve to give him up. In the end it was he who called a halt, breathing raggedly his face flushed with ill-concealed desire and sent her away, her body pulsing with arousal, her knees weak and her head and heart in a cloud.

iviana stumbled from the force of his hand on her lower back, propelling her into the room, and turned as she heard the door click shut and the sound of a key turning in the lock. Several candelabra were alight, the candles partially burned down as if they had been lit for a while. The room was dominated by a large, elaborately carved four-poster bed in dark wood, the covers dawn down invitingly. There was a large fire burning well, which had taken the chill off the air in the room. Spread out on a table, was a generous repast, laid for two.

With a thumping heart she said, "You planned this!"

"Of course," he said. "Although I didn't plan to do it with a hole in my shoulder." He sat down in one of the rooms two chairs. "Come here and dress my wound."

She stayed where she was, near the door, looking around the room. "Did you set those men on me?"

He smiled and waved her words aside. "I needed to frighten you a little, my dear."

"Why?" her heart beat a tattoo against her ribs.

"So that you would come with me of course. That's not

important now. Come here." He spoke imperatively and she felt suddenly very tired.

She approached him on legs that wobbled a bit. He put his good hand on her waist. "We will be married as soon as I can find a vicar, then I'll take you to the continent. You will like that." His good arm squeezed her and he said, "Dress my wound, then we can eat and go to bed, I warrant you're hungry and tired, I know I am."

She ignored this and began to unlace his shirt and to pull the sleeve away from the wound to expose the shoulder. The bleeding had slowed and was sluggish. It was a nasty slash and quite deep. The metallic tang of it made her swallow against a sudden wave of nausea. She filled the bowl with water from the ewer, and finding a towel, she began to wash the wound. The bloody water ran down his arm, further soaking his ruined shirt. He winced as she dabbed at the wound. "You should get this seen to by a doctor, it is quite deep and may require stitches," she said, turning away to find something to bandage him with.

"Well, we can have a doctor and a vicar as soon as the snow lifts. Until then, we will have to make do with each other, won't we?" he said, closing his eyes as she began winding a neck cloth round his shoulder to bandage the wound. She used a cravat pin to hold the bandage in place. Stepping back, she surveyed him, and he opened his eyes and looked at his shoulder. "Very neat. Now help me get this shirt off." He began to pull the shirt free of his breeches with his good hand, and she helped him pull one arm free and then pull it down off the wounded arm. His body was pale and his muscular chest was covered in a thick mat of curling dark hair, which arrowed down over his flat belly to the waistband of his tight-fitting breeches. His clothing had not been designed to cover any imperfections of form. She retreated, dropping the noisome garment in the corner, and turned back to find him standing in front of her, crowding her space and her senses. He still smelled of blood and her nose wrinkled against the odour. "I like you with more spirit my dear, what is the matter?"

She took a breath and stepped back. "I don't like the smell of blood," she admitted.

"Wash me then," he said. His eyes glittered in the candlelight.

She poured out some fresh water into a small bowl and washed away the dribbles of bloody water and smears of blood on his skin. She put the bowl aside with the cloth and moved to the fire, trying to keep distance between them, but he followed her and put his good arm round her pulling her against him. She put her hand on his chest and felt the roughness of the hairs under her fingers. He kissed her with the confidence of possession.

He tasted of brandy. She tried to pull away and his hand came up to the back of her skull and held her head where he wanted it. He didn't hurt her as he had done before, but his grip was firm. His lips grazed over her mouth and she held her lips firmly closed against his tongues attempt to part them. *Jack!* Her thoughts clung steadfastly to the memories of Jack's body pressing her into the tree, of his long hard length pressed against her back in the billiard room, of his lips on her neck. Tears seeped from under her lids, Jack was lost to her, she felt as if she had been fighting this man for an aeon.

She had wanted dangerous, now suddenly she had it, and it was horrifying. He lifted his head and she opened her eyes, assaulted by the liquid fire in his gaze. Jack had looked at her with similar molten longing. Her body shuddered, terrified of this man's strength. She had to fight him but how? His lips grazed her jaw line as his hand moved down her back, pressing her against him, and she felt the lump in his breeches pressing against her belly, hot and hard. He murmured against her throat "Viviana, you are a witch. I swear I love you!"

She gasped with revulsion as he kissed her neck, nipping the skin lightly with his teeth. "Anthony! —"

"Say you love me too!" he kissed her mouth possessively, his tongue invading in spite of her efforts to close her teeth against him. Revolted she tried to shove him away, and he groaned, a low rumble in his throat that made her shudder. He sank to his knees and buried his face in her belly, his breath hot through the fabric of her gown. He was breathing hoarsely and his shoulders shook. She looked down at his head in her hands bewildered.

He pressed his face between her legs, his lips and breath, hot through the cloth of her gown. He kissed her hard through her layers of petticoats. It was such an intimate unexpected thing to do, she clung to his head with her hands, her pelvis trapped against his face. She realised with a shock he'd got both hands on her buttocks pushing her against his face as he rubbed himself on her like a cat.

"Anthony -" she whispered shocked. "What -" He wrenched his head from her grip and said hoarsely, "It gets better love. Trust me." He got his feet under him and stood up clumsily, staggering. Relief that he had stopped his assault surged through her, and it was a moment before she realised, he was swaying dangerously. His skin was burning hot under her hands and his breathing harsh. A tentacle of hope wavered in her mind.

He staggered trying to keep his feet under him and sat down heavily in the chair by the table. "Food, let's eat my dear." He smiled and reached for the decanter to pour them each a goblet of wine. She sat reluctantly and reached for the wine with a hand that shook as he raised his goblet in toast. "To our future happiness my dear." She drank in silence watching him over the rim of her goblet.

His eyes glittered and his face was flushed, his brow and chest glistened with sweat, she could feel the heat pouring off him. He was burning up. How was he still upright? He reached for a bird and tore off a drumstick. He offered it to her, and she shook her head. "Ham then?" he said. Slicing some off the bone awkwardly with one hand and offering it to her. She nodded and he placed it on her plate, slicing off some for himself. She began to serve herself and him from the dishes laid out. Realising with a shock how hungry she was.

They ate in silence. She noticed that despite his initial enthusiasm he ate only sparingly and frequently wiped his brow with the napkin. He did drink the wine, refilling his goblet several times. When she sat back, replete, she realised he was watching her, like a cat, blinking in the light of the candelabra on the table.

"Had enough?" he asked, his voice was low and hoarse.

She nodded. "Thank you. You were right I was hungry."

He rose, swaying, unsteady on his feet and gripped the table to keep his balance. "Do you need to use the chamber pot? There is one behind that screen." He nodded to the corner of the room where a modesty screen stood. It was lacquered and painted with a Chinese design. She swallowed and nodded.

Emerging from behind the screen, having done her business, she saw that he had moved to the bed, where he sat.

"Come and remove my boots, I'm bloody useless thanks to you." He indicated his left arm which still hung like a dead sausage from his shoulder. She came and knelt to remove his boots. After tugging off first one and then the other, she set them aside and sat back on her heels to look up at him. He shivered convulsively.

"You have a fever."

"I do. But there is one thing I need to do first before I succumb," he gestured towards her, and she flinched.

He laughed. "No not that. I am not fit for that tonight, your virtue is safe my dear. I intend to be hale and hearty when I bed you. Come here."

She rose reluctantly, and he pulled her between his legs so that she stood with her breasts on a level with his eyes. Sweat rolled off his forehead into his eyes and he blinked, wiping it away with his right hand. "Put your hand on my good shoulder," he said.

"Why?"

"Just do it!" his tone becoming testy.

She obeyed reluctantly, wondering if the fever had over set his reason. Before she realised what he was about, he clamped a manacle around her wrist and closed it with a snap, pushing the pin home with his thumb. The other end of the manacle was attached by a chain about four feet in length to the newel post of the bed.

She pulled back with a cry. "What have you done? You beast, unchain me at once!"

He shook his head. "I'm sorry my dear, but I cannot risk losing you again, and I fear I'm not in any fit state to stop you should you choose to run."

She panted with fear and fury. "You monster! I should have killed you! Release me!" She hit out with her fists, and he ducked his head and put out a hand to catch her wrists. Even in his weakened condition he was still much stronger than her.

"Come to bed sweetheart, and sleep, you know you're exhausted." He shivered again and his teeth began to chatter. "D-damn!" he closed his eyes momentarily.

She pulled away from him as his grip loosened, and she called out. "Help! Someone please help me!"

He slewed around sinking back onto the bed and pulled the covers over himself murmuring, "It's no good calling out. The servants are well-trained. They won't help you. Come to bed." He shuddered under the covers.

She yanked at the manacle stretching the chain to its fullest extent and looked around wildly for something to break it with. There was nothing. The knife on the table was well out of reach. With an infuriated scream she picked up one of his boots and threw it at the wall in sheer frustration.

He opened one eye at the thud and laughed, it became a cough, and he went back to shivering under the covers. "Come to bed my beautiful termagant," he murmured.

"No, you bastard. I will never sleep with you!" With tears of fury and fear, streaming down her cheeks, she slid down onto the carpet beside the bed sobbing. She had brought this on herself, and she was truly lost now. Jack was gone, Denzil would recoil in horror from her and deservedly so. She was ruined. And it was all her won foolish fault. After knowing two such decent men as the Elliot brothers how could she reconcile herself to marrying this monster? She sobbed with fury and heart break.

"Suit yourself," breathed the monster on the bed above her.

IT WAS mid-afternoon when Jack cantered down the drive of Harcourt House and drew his horse to a halt at the front steps. The leaden sky made it seem like dusk. The windows stared blindly and the front door was ajar, almost as if the house were deserted. He dismounted and drew a pistol from the holster on his saddle. He approached the steps to the door cautiously. Peering round it, he saw a room across the hall with another open door. The vestibule was in shadow, gloomy with heavy dark wood panelling. The tiled floor showed a pair of muddy foot-prints, one large and one small set and a quantity of melt water pooled in the grout between the tiles. The house was eerily silent. He crossed the vestibule to the open door and came to an abrupt halt in the doorway.

A woman's cloak lay in a crumpled heap on the floor, a pair of duelling foils propped against a chair. The furniture was in disar ray, shoved out of the middle of the room, a glass stood on a side table with traces of liquor in it. The candles were guttered stubs, melted wax pooled around the base of the candle sticks. He moved into the room and caught a whiff of a metallic odour over the smell of candle wax and wood-smoke from the ashy fire that was all but out in the grate.

He looked around and saw a dark patch on the carpet.

Kneeling he touched it and his fingers came away damp and bloody. He stood, his heart thumping violently in his chest and his mind careening from one image of disaster to another. He picked up the cloak and shook it out, it showed marks of dirt and stains of melt water, the hem was grubby and sodden. He sniffed it and knew with certainty it was hers, the faint fragrance of lavender lingered on it and sent a rush of warmth to his belly. He turned and went back into the hall; squatting he examined the footprints. They showed a path that led into the room. But more faintly, they indicated one that led also from the room to the stairs.

He bounded up the stairs, his breath harsh in his ears, his heartbeat a steady drum in his chest. His throat ached with tension and a red haze threatened his vision. He surveyed the row of closed doors arranged down the hall. He tried several and the handles turned revealing empty rooms swathed in holland covers. The fourth door he tried was locked. He knocked and then thumped on it; rage, a barely controlled impulse, pounded in his blood.

"Harcourt! Open this door damn you, or I'll break it down!" His voice was hoarse with fury. His fists clenched with the desire to punch something, his muscles taught and quivering. He waited in the growing silence and resumed his thumping on the door, trying to decide if he could break the lock with his shoulder or shoot it out. Shooting would probably be better. He was just reaching for the pistol stuffed in the pocket of his great coat, when the door opened to reveal a tall, bare-chested man with a bandage wrapped round his shoulder, dressed only in breeches. He swayed dangerously, his skin glistened with sweat. His eyes were glazed, deep shadows beneath them, his face pale. He was breathing harshly.

"Harcourt?" the interrogative was purely form, Jack knew it was him.

He grinned baring his teeth. "You must be the brother. Captain Jack! You're trespassing you know."

"You left the front door open!" snarled Jack "Where is she?"

"Who?" responded the flame headed man weaving before him.

"Jack!" Viviana's voice made his heart skip and thud.

Jack lifted his booted leg and kicked the door open with the flat of his sole. It flew backwards, crashing on its hinges and Jack shouldered passed his host, pushing the man backwards into the room. Harcourt staggered slightly and propped himself against the wall watching, while Jack survey the room and took in the enormous bed, the table with the remnants of a meal for two and Viviana standing by the bed.

Her hair was tumbled about her face, which showed white and strained. Her gown was rumpled and stained with blood, and the hem was dirty and sodden. His heart turned over at the sight of her, what had happened to her?

"Jack!" she started towards him, and he saw the manacle on her wrist chaining her to the newel post of the bed. The chain brought her up short before she could reach him.

"Viviana!" horror skittled down his spine and his banked rage overflowed. He rounded on Harcourt "I'll kill you!"

"You're trespassing, get out of my house now!"

"Jack-" Viviana made another attempt to move towards him and Harcourt crossed the room and pulled her against him. She struggled visibly.

"Let her go! If you've hurt her -"

"She's my wife Elliot! There's nothing you can do! Get out of my house, now!" snapped Harcourt.

Jack stared at him, his mind racing. "Your wife?"

"You're too late Elliot. Married and bedded. She's mine, now get out, or I'll have you thrown out!"

Jack drew the pistol from his pocket and aimed it at Harcourt. "Not before I make her a widow!"

"Jack for God's sake don't kill him!" Viviana put out her hands.

With Jack's attention on her, Harcourt pulled her in front of him, pining her with one arm, using her as a shield. He spoke over her shoulder. "Put the gun down Elliot, you have no business here."

"Let her go!" said Jack.

Harcourt smiled and squeezed Viviana tighter. "Give up, Elliot she's mine. I told you that already. She's sampled my love making, and she likes it! Isn't that right sweetheart?" he said nuzzling her ear. She bit her lip and stayed silent, her eyes on the gun. Jack tried to catch her gaze, but she refused to look at him.

"Tell me something Harcourt, did you mean to kill my brother or just delay him?"

The effect of this was electric, Harcourt froze and Viviana gave a small shriek. She looked wildly at John. "Denzil's dead?"

Jack shook his head. "No, just a cracked skull." He met Harcourt's eyes deliberately. "He's being expertly nursed by Miss Anne Harcourt, you will be glad to know. They spent last night at the Bull and Bush, together, alone. Was that your idea Harcourt?"

Harcourt's colour changed and his breathing became more audible as he ground his teeth and Viviana whimpered as he squeezed her tighter. "What has he done to her?"

"Nothing. He's a gentleman, unlike you! You lying treacherous cur!" spat John. "Let go of her and fight me like a man!"

"I would, but you have me at a disadvantage," said Harcourt through his teeth. "The lady was before you. I underestimated her, she is an accomplished swords' mistress! Aren't you darling?" he squeezed her again and nibbled her ear. Viviana made a noise that could have been pleasure or annoyance. "Your brother could never have handled her, I've done him a favour you know! She is far too hot for him."

Jack tightened his hold on the pistol tempted to shoot anyway. His muscles were shaking with rage and tension. "Your sister gave me her permission to hurt you. I think I understand why! Only a coward hides behind a petticoat, injured or not. Let — her — go!" Jacks voice was ragged.

Harcourt shook his head and moved forward, pushing Viviana before him until they were facing Jack at point-blank range. He squeezed Viviana. "Take his gun!"

Jack, watching this manoeuvre, realised the full extent of Harcourt's injuries, he didn't have the use of his left arm. He was controlling Viviana purely with his right arm. She had her eyes trained on Jack, and she said steadily. "Jack, give me the gun." He tried to read her expression and failed. His mind raced. *Were they married, had Harcourt despoiled her? Was she willing or a hostage? She had begged him not to kill Harcourt.* He hesitated a long moment, his throat dry and his skin clammy.

He couldn't shoot Harcourt without running the risk of hurting her, even at this range.

He let the gun drop and stepped forward to offer it to her. She took it from him and Harcourt kissed her cheek. "Good girl". She looked up at him and smiled and Jack's felt as if he had been kicked in the stomach.

In the next moment she turned in Harcourt's arm as his grip slackened and she kneed him ferociously in the crotch, followed by a whack to his left shoulder with the butt of the gun. "That's for Lady, you bastard!" she said as he folded with a cry of pain, and she backed away from him with the gun trained on him in shaking hands. "Jack, get out of here!" she said her eyes still on the prone form of Harcourt who was writhing in pain on the floor.

Jack ignored her and moved round her to Harcourt. Bending over him, he dragged him up by the bandage and hit him flush to the jaw and dropped him. Harcourt sprawled, out cold. Jack turned and grabbed the gun from Viviana.

. . .

"Where's the key to that thing?" Jack nodded at the chain.

"I don't know," they spent the next few minutes searching for it. She found it under one of the pillows on the bed. In moments, she was free of the manacle and rubbing her reddened wrist. She looked round as the cocking of the gun warned her.

Jack stood with the gun aimed at Harcourt's prone form on the floor.

"Jack don't! We're not married! He was lying to you. Don't kill him, please!" Her heart thudded in her chest and her legs trembled. "He didn't hurt me apart from the chain. Please, Jack, don't ruin your life for me, I'm not worth it."

Jack lowered the gun slowly and looked over at her. His face was ravaged with a look she had never seen before. His eyes looked haggard. "He didn't touch you?"

She shook her head, swallowing the ache in her throat. "He was too ill, with fever. I pinked him with a foil in the shoulder," she nodded at the bandage.

Jack stared at her and whatever showed in her face made him uncock the gun and place it in his great coat pocket before crossing the floor and pulling her into his arms and kissing her. It was a hard ravaging kiss that blasted through all her defences, raw and needy and possessive. Relief and desire made her melt in his arms and tears start to her eyes. A sob escaped her round the kiss, and he released her mouth and hugged her close.

"I'm sorry, I'm a beast!" he said roughly. "You've been through hell, and I'm ravishing you like a boor."

"No!" she swallowed. "Don't apologise, I like it!"

"Do you?" he gave her a wry quizzical smile.

She put a hand up to his face and stroked his bristly cheek. "I thought I'd never see you again!"

"I'm never letting you out of my sight again!" His voice was hoarse with emotion and weariness. His hands tight on her waist. "I could shake you whatever possessed–no never mind we need to get out of here before he wakes up!" he nodded at Harcourt on the floor and took her hand dragging her to the door.

They raced down the stairs, at the bottom she said, "My cloak!" and dashed into the room to grab it off the floor. They fled to the door, down the steps, to where Tempest stood waiting. He kissed her hard once more and flung her onto the horse, stowed the pistol and swung into the saddle in front of her.

"Hold tight!" he said as he turned Tempest and kicked him into a gallop down the drive. She wrapped her arms round his waist, pressing her cheek against his back. She was shaking with reaction and the tears she had been battling, rose up threatening to choke her. He covered one of her hands with his and set Tempest at the gate.

CHAPTER 23

*C*linging to Jack, her face buried in the rough cloth of his heavy great coat, Viviana swayed with the motion of the cantering horse as they rode cross-country. She lost track of time, only rousing when he slowed the horse and brought it to a halt. By the position of the sun, it was late afternoon. Dismounting, he reached up and lifted her from the saddle, setting her gently on her feet in the shelter of his arm. She looked round dazedly in the lengthening shadows.

They had stopped by a ramshackle building set back from the road. He led her and the horse towards it, pushing the door open enough to permit their entry. It was a barn. A shaft of light from the westering sun illuminated enough of the interior to show some loose hay and a few bails stacked in a corner and some farming implements against the walls. It smelt of hay and dirt and musty dampness. She was so exhausted she didn't care.

He led her to the hay, took off his coat and laid it down and then removed her cloak. "Lie down, rest, I'll guard you." His kindness after the terrors and barrage of abuse she had sustained for the last thirty-six hours, brought the tears to her eyes again, and she flung herself against his chest and wept. He stroked her hair and held her. His breath warm on her face as he kissed the top of her head and murmured meaningless, comforting things. As her first flood of tears subsided, he tried to move away, but she clung to him stubbornly. "Hold me! Please."

His voice sounded strained as he said, "All right, but lie down. It's cold." He lowered them gently into the hay and pulled her cloak over them. "Sleep." He said quietly over her head. She nuzzled her face into his chest and for the first time in hours let her body truly relax. Her feet were frozen, but his body offered heat and safety and between the heavy, insulating cloth of his coat beneath them, and her cloak over them, they created a cocoon of warmth into which she burrowed with deep relief.

Eventually she said, "How did you find me?" her head was pillowed on his upper arm and her hands against his chest, as they lay face to face, their bodies separated by some space below the waist for decencies' sake. His arms held her, but he kept his hands circumspectly on her shoulders and upper back. She was acutely conscious of their physical proximity and knew he must be too. She could feel him quivering, and she was pretty sure it had nothing to do with the cold. He was so long answering her, she thought he wasn't going to, but eventually he told her about Mary's letter and finding Denzil at the Inn with Anne.

"Is he very angry with me?"

"Hurt I think, more than anything," replied Denzil's brother.

She sighed, and he said as if the words were torn from him. "Why did you do it? Where were you going?"

She lifted her head. "To you of course, in London."

The light that came in through the door showed enough of his face for her to see his expression. It was part joy and part exasperation. "You're mad!" He said with conviction, but there was a warmth in his voice that made her heart lift.

"I know" she said in a small voice. "And I'm sorry, but I

couldn't bear the idea that you would go back to the continent and I might never see you again."

"A letter would have done, love," he said in a thickened voice.

"I didn't think of that," she said contritely.

"You didn't think at all!" he said exasperated.

"Oh, shut up and kiss me Jack," said Miss Torrington. His lips found her hers, and she parted them for his deep, lingering, assaulting kiss. Emerging from the onslaught she said dreamily. "Oh yes."

"I've been wanting to kiss you since I first laid eyes on you," he confessed moving closer.

"I know," she said moving even closer. "I've been wanting you to."

"Viviana?" he said hovering over her mouth, his thigh pressing against hers.

"Hm?" she asked drinking him in with her eyes and lining up her mouth for another kiss.

"What happened to you? What did that bastard do to you?"

She closed her eyes and shuddered. "I don't want to talk about it."

He pulled back and moved one of his hands to her upper arm. "What did he do? Tell me! Did he hurt you?"

She opened her eyes and surveyed his face, looking for a clue as to how to tell him what happened without upsetting him. "A bit, once or twice," she admitted. "But" she added as he was about to say something, "Considering how much I hurt him, probably not more than I deserved."

He stared at her intently and said slowly, "I don't think I understand. What do you mean?"

"Well, I bit him, and I stabbed him with the duelling foil and I kneed him in the crotch twice, and I hit his wound twice too." She said ticking these incidences off with her fingers. "Oh, and I pushed him over so that he cracked his head on the side of the table." She added remembering this last injury.

"And why was all this violence necessary?" asked Jack grimly.

"Well, he was doing his damnedest to seduce me you see."

"I gather he didn't succeed?" said Jack, his eyes scanning her face.

"No, he didn't!"

Jack shifted, taking his weight on one arm, and pinning her forearm with his other hand, and her eyes with his. "How close did he get?"

She swallowed her heart thumping quickly and stared up into his eyes, which had darkened with that possessive half-crazy look he'd given her in Anthony's bedchamber. Her body shifted under his, warmth blooming between her legs. She reached for him but he moved away.

"God Viviana!" he said in a voice that sounded stricken.

She sat up looking at his shoulder and the back of his head. "Jack, he didn't ravish me! I didn't let him."

"He didn't rape you. I can see that. He wanted you to come to him willingly, didn't he?"

She stared at his back and finally she said, "Yes. That was what he wanted."

"And you almost did, didn't you?" The harshness in his voice made her flinch.

"No! It wasn't like that, " she protested.

He rounded on her, kneeling on their makeshift bed "Oh yes it was! What would have happened if I hadn't come when I did? What did I interrupt in that big bed of his? How far had he got?"

She scrambled to her knees and slapped him. "How dare you!" Tears started hot to her eyes and spilled down her cheeks. "I fought him with everything I had, but he wouldn't stop! He w-wouldn't stop!" She flung at him furiously, beating at him with her hands, the past hours of pent-up emotion flooding out. "He kept kissing me and talking to me, telling me he loved me! And lady b-broke her leg!" She stopped, hiccoughing with sobs and buried her face in her hands. "And I'm so -sorry!"

. . .

"No Viviana, I'm sorry!" He said gathering her up. He closed his eyes over her head and rocked her, a hard, cold stone in his chest, where there had been burning jealousy moments before.

She sobbed into his chest for the second time that night and blubbered, "He sent the dogs to chase me d-down. That's how lady broke her leg! And then he told me it was *my* f-fault!"

The stone split, as if sundered by a lightning strike of anger, so strong it almost took his breath away. He gasped "He set the dogs on you?"

She nodded, snuffling into his shirt, and gulping for breath. "I got away on Lady, and he chased me down with his dogs. I was terrified and Lady missed her footing and broke her leg!" She shook her head.

"Shooting is too good for that bastard! I'll kill him with my bare hands!" said Jack, his voice thick with vengeance.

She shook her head wearily. "Just take me home. I'm so tired!" She wiped her face as another tear spilled over. "He said he would break me. I think he has." She shivered convulsively.

Jack gathered her close, pulling her down under the covers and said quietly, "Sleep a little, then I'll take you home. You're safe now. I won't let him near you again. Ever."

She sniffed and settled herself. He stroked her hair and stared at the shadowed wall. Gradually he felt her relax, her body curled against his, her breath soft against his neck. He couldn't sleep, he was too keyed up, with emotion and the fact of her nearness. He had dreamed of holding her in his arms, but never of the circumstances that would lead to it. He kept living over and over those moments when he had the gun trained on Harcourt and wished he had pulled the trigger. *If he had known -!*

Tempest moved about in the dark, lipping at the loose hay, his bridle clinking. The horse needed brushing down and watering.

He would let her sleep a little longer, and then they would press on to the Inn, he would leave her there with Denzil and go back and throttle that bastard. He spent some time relieving his feelings, imaging that scenario.

She moved in her sleep, and he became suddenly and acutely aware of her body pressed against him and the effect it was having on his. Thoughts of murder turned to love, and he took in a hissing breath, as he held himself still against the exquisite surge of lust diving down his spine and settling in his groin. He tried to think of other things but found his hands wandering without volition. She stirred again and in the next instant he found her mouth under his. He sank helpless into the kiss, drawn by a magnet more powerful than gravity.

Lifting his head reluctantly he said in a voice gone thick with lust, "Viviana love, stop, I haven't the strength to resist you."

She touched his face with her hands. "Jack, do you love me?"

He gave a sort of choked laugh. "Viviana a man in this state would say anything! But yes, God help, me I love you. From the first moment I saw you, I think. I was so jealous of Den and so angry with you for hurting him -"

She closed her eyes and whispered, "Poor Denzil, I feel terrible about that!"

"Well, I wouldn't feel too terrible, love. I hate to bruise your ego, but I think he is fast recovering."

"What do you mean?" she asked, opening her eyes wider.

"I rather think he has fallen for red hair and a pair of green eyes. It's not like Den to be so fickle. I fear the blow to his head has addled his brain rather badly."

She sat up. "What are you talking about?"

He rolled onto his back, pillowing his head on his arms and regarded her offended profile. "I mean that my respectable brother has been caught by the cleverest mantrap I've ever seen. Harcourt's sister, Anne."

"You think she was set to trap him by Anthony?"

Her use of Harcourt's Christian name made him twitch internally, but he suppressed the feeling. "I don't know. Den vehemently maintains her innocence, but I'm not so sure. The circumstances look suspiciously coincidental, and I dislike coincidence as a means of explanation."

"Is she beautiful, this Anne?" asked Viviana, turning to look at him.

"Not my style," he said touching her face with a gentle finger. "Striking rather than beautiful, her features are uneven, but her colouring is startling. She is, I would hazard a guess, an acquired taste. Not my taste anyway. But she may well be Den's. He seemed very taken with her."

She lowered her eyes. "I see".

He sat up and took her chin in his hand, forcing her eyes up. "Piqued, to have lost an admirer?"

She pulled away and said lightly. "Of course not! It's a great relief if he has indeed found a lady worthy of him. But if she is a mantrap, then I am concerned for Den!" she pulled the cloak around her shoulders shivering. "And if she is Anthony's sister, how can she be anything else?" Her face twisted and she said softly, "I have brought disaster on us all by my thoughtless, wilful, stupidity!"

He pulled her closer until she was curled between his legs and wrapped his arms round her. "We're none of us perfect my darling."

"You are!" she said with a smile, resting her head on his upper arm and regarding him with a melted expression.

"You're besotted!" he said roughly.

"Yes, I am" she admitted, touching his cheek with her hand. He bent his head and kissed her again, rolling her back onto the hay. After a bit he said thickly, "We had better resume our journey, or I'm going to have you here and now!"

. . .

SHE SAID SOFTLY, "Don't tempt me Jack, I'm a lit firecracker!" She kissed his jaw, her hands pulling him closer. He made a muffled noise and kissed her again, pressing her into the hay with his body. She arched under him, pressing closer, his leg had got between hers and the long-banked fire of their attraction exploded in her body. Her nipples ached and the heat between her legs throbbed as she moaned low in her throat and covered his face with kisses, her hands grabbing at his shirt, pushing it up so that she could touch his chest and stomach and back.

"Don't" he said thickly even as he pushed her bodice down and rained kisses over her skin, cradling one breast in his hand and lowering his head to touch one taught nipple with his tongue.

She hissed in a breath and whispered "Oh yes" she pressed her pelvis against him feeling the heat and hardness of him through their clothing. They rocked against one another as his tongue worked over her nipple and she arched her neck and her back, revelling in giving into the feelings she had been holding in check for so long. She was hot and wet and -

He groaned pushing up her skirts. "Heaven's gate, the sooner I marry you the better."

"Oh good," she said. "I was beginning to wonder if you would ever ask!"

"Ask? God Viviana, will you have me? I'm a soldier and a younger son, I've no title or fortune, except what I can make myself. Your family won't like it. I'm not half the catch Den is."

"Since when have I ever cared what others think?" she asked indignantly.

"True," he said kissing her. "I should probably sell out."

"Not unless you want to. I fancy living in a tent," she said smiling.

"That's only because you know nothing about it! It's cold, wet, and damnably uncomfortable."

"I wouldn't mind if I had you to keep me warm." She said stroking his chest.

"CAN YOU WRING A CHICKEN'S NECK?" he asked trying to suppress another groan.

She narrowed her eyes. "You're teasing me. I'd learn.

Whatever it takes Jack. You cannot fault my courage!" She rubbed her face on his chest like a cat.

"No, that I can't" he admitted his hands wandering under her skirts.

"I'm brave enough for anything except to sit at home and wait for you. I couldn't do that." She said with pain in her eyes. "Don't make me do that. I would die."

"All right I won't make you do that" he agreed and kissed her.

She arched against him with a moan and the last vestiges of his self-control snapped. "Viviana," he groaned against her neck nipping the soft skin and making her shiver.

"Jack," she panted, her hips rolling, pressing herself closer against his aching erection. "Please!"

His wandering hand reached the apex of her legs and discovered the wet sticky folds of her sex. Sliding a finger between her swollen lips he elicited a groan from her and shuddered. The surge of mind-bending desire that had overtaken him in the billiard room came back with a rush and his cock jerked with the force of it. She gasped pushing up into his touch, all instinct and pleading, passionate desire.

"God Jack!" she said, her voice low and aching.

His hips thrust against her pelvis involuntarily as his fingers explored her flesh and his mouth made a meal of her neck and breasts. He swirled his fingers over her bud of pleasure and rubbed gently, making her arch and moan and shudder. He thrust a finger inside her, and she gasped arching up against his touch.

"Is that what you want?" he panted low and hoarse.

"Yes! More! Please, more." He added a second finger and thrust hard and deep feeling her jerk and her voice catch on a cry. "Jack, oh God, I need you please..." He shuddered the sharpness of his desire almost painful and impossible to resist. He pushed her gown up out of the way and fumbled with the buttons of his falls. His aching cock, released from its prison, twitched and leaked. He shifted position rolling between her legs, seeking the place to drive into her and slake their mutual desire.

He lifted his head to catch her eyes and she jerked and cried out below him as he slid inside her, her legs gripping him tightly, panting and flushed, her eyes wild. He bent and kissed her, thrusting his tongue into her mouth with hungry passionate desire. She pushed up into his downward thrust, and he drove them both towards the precipice with rapid brutal strokes. She jerked again, stiffened under him and her face suffused with incandescent bliss as the wave hit and took her under. His own crested and with the last of his self-control he wrenched free of her tight heat and spent his seed between her legs. The pleasure washed like a wave through his body and he collapsed on her breathless and boneless with release.

God, what had he done? Behaved like a beast... He lay listening to his heavily thumping heartbeat and getting his breath back, she lay under him her legs loosened, her breath hot against his ear.

"You have to marry me now," he said softly.

"Yes Captain Elliot," she breathed. "Thank you," she added.

"You're welcome," he murmured kissing her neck. With an effort he rolled off her. "I didn't mean to be such a beast," he added. "Not for your first time." He lifted his head to look at her.

She smiled and kissed him. "A beast was what I needed. You have leave to be a beast as often as you like."

"Really?" he grinned and dipped his head to her bosom, giving a nipple another kiss. She sighed and arched up into him.

He sighed in return. "Just as soon as I've had some sleep.

I've been awake for the better part of forty- eight hours." He closed his eyes and rolled sideways pulling her close and in moments he was asleep.

VIVIANA LOOKED at him and her heart swelled. Yes, she had finally chosen the right man.

CHAPTER 24

*A*nne sat up with a start, blinking and trying to make her eyes penetrate the darkness of her bedchamber. Her heart thumped heavily in her ears and her stomach dropped with fluttery anticipation, *was she dreaming?* "Whose there?" she said huskily, clutching the coverlet in hands gone clammy with mingled fright and hope.

A large shadow moved, and she felt the mattress sink under his weight. "It's me, don't squawk and wake the whole household!"

She sank back against the pillows crossly. "Anthony! What are you doing, creeping about in the middle of the night!" she sat up again. "And what are you doing here anyway! I thought you were visiting friends?" She looked around, feeling a cold draught and saw the window sash was wide and the curtains billowing in the night breeze "And why in heaven's name did you break into my room through the window?"

"I said don't screech!" he repeated softly. "I need your help."

"Oh, do you?" said Anne darkly. "What have you done with the beauty?"

"What do you know about that?" he asked suspiciously.

"Not much, except that I gather you have run off with Denzil's affianced bride" snapped Anne.

"And since when did he become Denzil to you?"

"Since you knocked him on the head and left him to die in the snow! It was you, wasn't it? Did you mean for him to freeze to death, or just for me to run him down with my coach?" she said, her voice thickening with suppressed tears. "You're a monster Anthony I don't know how I bear with you!"

"In fact, you finding him was a fortuitous accident. I didn't plan that, but it couldn't have been better in the circumstances," he replied quietly, robbing her momentarily of speech. "Now listen, I need you to -"

Finding her voice, she put her hands over her ears. "No! I'm not listening to anything!"

He took her hands away from her ears and held them one handed. "Anne, you will -"

She shrugged off his grip emphatically. "No, I won't! I don't care what you want Anthony, I'm not helping you!"

The moon came out from behind a cloud just then and sent a shaft of light into the room onto his face, and she gasped. "Good God what happened to you?"

"Look a bit the worse for wear, do I?" he asked wearily. She reached out to raise the shutter on the night-lamp and turn the wick up. Turning back to him in the sudden flare of light, she took in the full impact of his bruised face and his useless left hand lying slack on his knee.

He looked down at himself deprecatingly and said with a heavy slice of irony, "Viviana happened to me largely." He fingered his jaw. "Although this I can attribute to Captain Elliot. I gather you have met him?"

Anne nodded, distracted by his left arm as she reached out to touch him. "I told him he could hurt with my good wishes, but not to kill you!"

"Thank you for the consideration dear sister!"

"What do you mean: Viviana happened to you? Did she do this?" She lifted his hand and let it drop gently back to his thigh.

He winced. "Yes. Miss Torrington, it turns out, is an accomplished sword's mistress, which I learnt to my cost."

Anne sat back and stifled a laugh, covering her mouth with her hand.

"It's not funny!" said her aggrieved brother.

Anne gasped. "Yes, it is." She swallowed and tried to get her face under control and gave up at his look of hurt pride, going off into a peel of laughter. "Serves you right Anthony, I'm sure you deserved it."

He rubbed his face with his good hand and said glumly, "Probably. In fact, you're right. I've lost her. And I was so close — if I hadn't succumbed to that fever and Elliot hadn't arrived when he did -" His jaw tightened.

"What is the attraction Anthony, her beauty or her fortune?" asked Anne cynically.

"Both," he said frankly. "I need the money desperately. But the real irony is this, and no doubt it will make you laugh even harder at my expense, I actually love her." He looked down at his inert hand and went on. "It's the strangest emotion. I did some terrible things to her, and she fought me every step of the way. I could master her if I had just a little longer." He swallowed and looked at Anne. "I don't suppose you believe me?"

Anne frowned at him. "I've no doubt you believe yourself. But if you hurt her, I don't see how you can say you love her."

"Don't you?" he smiled an ironic smile "But we always hurt those most that we care for, don't we?"

Anne looked away and said quietly, "Not all of us, no."

"Then you are more fortunate than I knew Anne." He took her hand and squeezed it lightly. Letting it go he said, "God I'm getting maudlin, I'll be apologising to *you* next!"

"Don't strain yourself brother! Or I'll have a fit of the vapours, and then you'll look no how!" said Anne tartly, surreptitiously wiping away a tear.

He smiled. "You? Vapours? You would no more have a fit of swooning than Viviana would. I don't think I have fully appreciated you sister, until this moment."

She shook her head. "I am not going to help you, Anthony. Stop it. You can't cozen your way round me. Especially after you kicked me out of my own home!"

"That stung, did it?"

She looked at him and said nothing.

"I'm sorry, I was in a foul mood that day, I had just found out Viviana had accepted Stanton's suit. I didn't mean it you know."

"Oh yes you did! You're a beast when you're in a temper. You also told me, no man of sense would have me! Well let me tell you again, no woman of breeding would have you!" said Anne thumping her pillows and sitting back against them with her arms crossed under her bosom.

"Seems to me, we've both changed. You used to be a demure little thing, what happened?" Anne flushed and looked away.

"Stanton?" he probed.

"Lord Stanton has nothing to do with it" said Anne with dignity. "I just decided to stand up for myself. I'm tired of being a doormat!"

"Stanton." He said again. He looked at her thoughtfully. "What's been happening here? You've been at this Inn with him for what, a day and half? Has he been making love to you Anne?" She flushed scarlet. "Certainly not!"

"I think I might need to have a word with him in that case," said her brother purposefully.

"Don't you dare!" said Anne springing at him like a cat. He shook her off and stood up. She scrambled out of bed and followed him. "Anthony, no! For God's sake, what are you going to do?"

"Defend my sisters honour of course! What else?" he said

looking down at her.

She looked at him helplessly. "Anthony, I'm begging you, don't do this!"

THE SOUND of voices penetrated Denzil's slumber, and he was suddenly wide awake. He traced the sound that had disturbed him to Anne's room. Sitting up with his heart thumping heavily, he listened and caught the low tone of a masculine voice and the higher tones of Anne's. He couldn't make out the words but the urgent, anxious tenor of Anne's had him out of bed in an instant. The fire in the grate had died down and the air was chilly. He pulled on his breeches but didn't bother to tuck in the shirt he had been making serve double duty as a nightshirt. Picking up the pistol by his bed, he stuffed it in the waistband of his breeches and trod quietly on bare feet to the door and opened it carefully. Anne's room was next to his and shared a common wall and chimney.

The hall was empty, meagre light provided by a dimmed night lamp on a table between the doors of the two rooms. The door to Anne's room was closed, was it locked? He stopped and listened. The voices had dropped, and he still couldn't make out what was being said, but it was clear that one voice belonged to a man and that Anne wasn't happy with whatever he was saying.

Denzil's head was pounding with the pulse of his heartbeat, as he set his hand on the polished wooden doorknob and tried to turn it carefully. He expected it to be locked and was not surprised when it resisted his attempt to turn it but was taken aback when it turned in the other direction under his hand and the door opened, and he found himself toe to toe with Anthony Harcourt.

He caught a glimpse of Anne over her brother's shoulder, an expression of horror on her face, before Harcourt claimed his full attention with a venomous snarl.

"Lecherous Cur!" Harcourt reached out and grabbed Stanton's shirt, hauling him into the room. The two men were of similar height, although Harcourt was broader and more solidly built.

Stanton got his feet under him and pulled out of Harcourt's grasp saying quickly, "It's not what you think! I heard a man's voice in Miss Harcourt's room, I came to check that she was safe!"

"Liar!" growled Harcourt lunging at him with his right fist.

Anne shrieked, "Anthony don't!" and Stanton danced out of Harcourt's reach.

Harcourt rounded on her. "Stop trying to protect your lover, strumpet!"

"That's enough!" said Stanton. "I don't care if you are her brother, you won't speak to her like that in my presence! Miss Harcourt is entirely innocent. If you have any issue, you will address it to me, Sir!"

"Denzil please don't," whimpered Anne, her hands to her mouth.

Ignoring her, Denzil glared at Harcourt who bared his teeth. "With pleasure Stanton. Which is it to be, swords or pistols?" he asked his eyes never wavering from Denzil's face.

Anne gasped and Denzil replied steadily "Your choice Harcourt." His pulse thumped.

"Considering I'm hors de combat, perhaps pistols would be fairer, don't you think?" he said indicating his left arm, which Denzil realised with a shock was hanging uselessly at his side.- Denzil nodded. "As you wish. Do you have a weapon?"

Harcourt reached into the pocket of his great coat and produce a pistol. "Do you?"

Denzil showed his own. "Outside?"

"Certainly"

"Are you mad?" said Anne staring at them. "It's the middle of the night!"

"It's a full moon" said Stanton "After you Harcourt," he said, holding the door.

Harcourt preceded him and Anne snatched up her cloak and followed "Stop this insanity! Denzil for God's sake -"

He turned. "You should stay here, it's not appropriate -"

"I'm coming!" said Anne her eyes flashing green fire. "He's my brother! Denzil don't do this please!"

He looked at her sadly. "I must Anne. I'm sorry, but he has impugned my honour to the point that I cannot ignore it!"

"This is about Miss Torrington, isn't it? Not me?" she said in a low voice.

"Both!" said Stanton turning away and following Harcourt down the stairs.

ANNE FOLLOWED both men down the stairs and out into the stable yard. Her hands were shaking, and she shivered with the cold air and the lump of fear in the pit of her stomach. She approached her brother and said in a low voice,

"Anthony on our mothers grave, for God's sake, stop this!"

He glanced at her and went back to checking his pistol. "Go stand over there and keep quiet," he nodded at the stable wall with his head.

She put her hand on his arm and began, "Anthony -"

"I said shut up and get out of the way!" She took a step back from his brutal hostility.

Denzil looked up from his own gun. "Please Anne, stay out of the way, you're a distraction for both of us." His tone was gentler than her brothers, but it was clear his intent was as fixed.

With a shudder she went to stand where he indicated, unable to stop tears from welling up. She fought to stifle them as she stood hugging her arms in the cold and watching both men make their preparations.

The yard was white with firm packed snow several inches

thick. Drifts of it piled against the stable and Inn walls. The moons silvered light shone brightly, reflected back by the whiteness of the snow. The contrast between light and deep shadow was strong. The snow blanketed sound too, so the whole scenario was eerily quiet.

She watched in fascinated horror as the two men came together each with a pistol in his hand, bowed and turned to stand with their backs to one another. Stanton said coolly,

"On a count of three, ten paces, turn and fire, yes?"

"Agreed" replied Harcourt steadily.

"One. Two. Three," counted Stanton, his voice like a drum beat in the night.

Anne counted the paces in her head as each man strode out, their booted feet crunching on the snow, their breath cloudy in the cold air, each step a hammer blow to her heart... eight...nine...ten!

Each man turned and raised his arm, took aim and Anne, unable to stand still and witness in silence, screamed and raced forward into the path of their aim. With a cry Stanton's arm jerked up and Anne felt the hot burn of a bullet hit her shoulder, her legs buckled, and she crumpled to the ground.

JACK HEARD the shot and rounded the corner of the building on Tempest, Viviana clinging to his waist.

A cloaked figure lay in the snow and over it hovered his brother and *Satan alive! Harcourt.* Flinging himself from the saddle, Jack ran towards the group, his breath rasping cold air in his throat. "God what happened here?"

At the same time, people began pouring out of the Inn, a stout woman, and a younger version of herself. Two lads came out of the stable. Jack ignored them and came to a halt by his brother's side. He was kneeling in the snow and had Miss Harcourt in his arms. Blood spread in a dark cloud from her shoulder. Her face was waxen and her eyes closed, her lashes a dark smudge on her cheeks.

Jack, with a sound like an enraged dog, turned and seized Harcourt and took a swipe at him. Harcourt shook his head like a stunned bull and dodged the blow, backing up, he held up his good arm to ward off another blow and kicked out with a leg aiming for Jack's crotch. Jack avoided the contact at the last moment by turning side on and seized Harcourt's injured arm and brought him to his knees by twisting it up his back. With a cry of pain, Harcourt buckled, sweat breaking out on his face and Jack held him down panting.

"What happened here?" he gasped, aware of Viviana hovering close. He looked to his brother who was sitting in the snow with Miss Harcourt, his shirt covered in blood, the bandage from his head over one eye and looking so thoroughly disreputable, that Jack almost laughed.

"He shot her!" said Denzil in the oddest voice. "She ran between us and he shot her!"

Jack looked down at the man in his hands and shook him. "You are the veriest cur!" he spat. Harcourt had his head down and wasn't looking at either of them.

Viviana knelt beside Denzil and put her hand on Anne's neck. "She is still alive. Come we should get her inside."

Denzil picked up Anne's limp form and carried her swiftly into the Inn, past the landlady's stunned form. As if this activity released her from her frozen shock Mrs Kennedy followed him in, berating them for heathen madmen. Denzil ignored her. Viviana followed and told her to be quiet. Jack smiled and hauled Harcourt to his feet. His hands clenched, he said in a low tone, "I should wring your neck and dump you in a snow drift you bastard!"

Harcourt looked at him dully. "Feel free, I won't stop you."

Jack eyed him with loathing. "What you did to Miss Torrington was unforgivable. What kind of man are you?"

"A desperate one," responded Harcourt in a voice Jack didn't recognise. Harcourt twisted suddenly and punched Jack in the stomach with his good arm. Jack double up with a grunt and lost his grip on Harcourt's arm.

Harcourt put some distance between them and waited for Jack to straighten. "For the record," he said, "I didn't mean to shoot her, she got in the way at the last minute."

"You had just better pray she doesn't die!" said jack circling him.

"I do." Harcourt took a breath and cleared his throat as if something were choking him. His eyes shifted and Jack heard Viviana's voice behind him.

"You had better not kill him, Jack."

Jack's back tightened and he said, "Give me one good reason why not."

"Well, I think he is going to be your brother-in-law for one thing. It's a flesh wound; with nursing she will be fine." Jack saw the relief in Harcourt's eyes and the tension go out of his shoulders.

"Viviana!" Harcourt spoke to her across Jack. She came forward until she was level with Jack, and he could see her face. "I'm sorry," said Harcourt.

Viviana took a breath. "What for?"

"All of it. But particularly for Lady." She swallowed and nodded.

Harcourt straightened and bowed to Jack. "I'll relieve you all of my presence. Tell my sister…." He stopped and took a breath. "Tell her I love her."

He turned and walked over to his horse, untied it from the railing, mounted and rode out of the yard while Jack stood and watched him, dumbfounded.

He turned to look at Viviana who walked straight into his arms and kissed him.

CHAPTER 25

$\mathcal{A}$nne stirred and opened her eyes. She was lying in bed and her shoulder hurt. There was an early morning light making its way through the curtains. Her night gown was ripped at the neck and her hand encountered a cloth bandage over her shoulder. She looked up and found Denzil standing by her bed.

She smiled at him, and he sat making the mattress sink and took her hand. "Are you better?" he asked.

"Did I dream it?"

He shook his head, lacing his fingers tightly with hers

"No. I think that was the worst moment of my life."

She smiled again. "I think it was the best of mine."

"Anne if you ever do anything so crazy again -"

"Yes?" she grinned "What will you do?"

"My dearest promise me you never will!"

"Where is Anthony?" she asked.

"Jack refrained from killing him. It was the considered opinion that if he was to be my brother-in-law it wouldn't be seemly to kill him or hand him over to a constable."

Anne's heart turned over and she said breathlessly, "Oh! Well, I'm glad of that."

"He said to tell you that he loved you" added Denzil.

Anne dropped her eyes, blinking against sudden tears she said softly, "Oh Anthony!"

He squeezed her hand gently in silence for a moment and then went on a little diffidently, "Jack is going to marry Viviana you know. So, I'm officially jilted. We thought we might have a double wedding, just to give the gossips something to talk about. What do you think?"

"Oh Denzil!" said Anne in quite a different voice.

The Earl of Stanton kissed her tenderly. "I gather that is a yes?"

Miss Anne Harcourt flung her good arm round his neck.

"Oh Yes Denzil!"

THE END

ACKNOWLEDGMENTS

I would like to thank my beta readers who made this book so much better. And a particular shout out to Gloria for her constructive feedback and for reading and rereading the subsequent draft, and also for helping me to craft a beautiful cover. Thank you to the members of the Ton and the Tartan's and the Historical Romance Book Club for feedback and comments on the cover and the blurb.

ALSO BY WREN ST CLAIRE

The Assassin's Wife

The Missing Heir

Book 2 in the Villains Redemption Series

Taming the Devil

Sir Anthony Harcourt is now the Duke of Mowbray, but with the title comes a mountain of debt and a reckoning, as the sins of his grandfather come crashing down upon him in the form of a beautiful virago bent on revenge and obtaining what is hers.

Miss Diana Lovell is a desperate woman. She blames the late Duke of Mowbray for her father's death and ruining her life. She reasons that the current Duke is cut from the same cloth as his grandsire and she means to get what is hers by right from him, no matter the cost.

Passion explodes when these two souls collide and bitter, cynical Anthony discovers that love may be possible after all, if he can only redeem himself sufficiently to deserve it.

Made in the USA
Monee, IL
27 November 2023

47564177R00132